Also by Geoffrey Household

Novels

THE THIRD HOUR

ROGUE MALE

ARABESQUE

THE HIGH PLACE

A ROUGH SHOOT

A TIME TO KILL

FELLOW PASSENGER

WATCHER IN THE SHADOWS

THING TO LOVE

OLURA

Autobiography

AGAINST THE WIND

Short Stories

THE SALVATION OF PISCO GABAR

TALES OF ADVENTURERS

THE BRIDES OF SOLOMON

SABRES ON THE SAND

For Children

THE SPANISH CAVE

The
Courtesy of Death

The
Courtesy of Death

❖

a novel by

GEOFFREY HOUSEHOLD

An Atlantic Monthly Press Book

LITTLE, BROWN AND COMPANY · BOSTON · TORONTO

ATLANTIC–LITTLE, BROWN BOOKS
ARE PUBLISHED BY
LITTLE, BROWN AND COMPANY
IN ASSOCIATION WITH
THE ATLANTIC MONTHLY PRESS

Published simultaneously in Canada
by Little, Brown & Company (Canada) Limited

PRINTED IN THE UNITED STATES OF AMERICA

The
Courtesy of Death

I HAD never thought of the bungalow as lonely. It was separated from The Green Man by only thirty yards of straggling roses and lawn and all the showy annuals which you find in a pub garden. Its other side faced a cart track beyond which was an abandoned yard, grass and nettles growing through the paving, where former stables and a half-roofless coach house formed an L-shaped block.

I was sitting up doing accounts in the kitchen, because the light was better. In the other room the lamp was so placed that only in bed could you see to read or write. It was after twelve, and a man coming down from the hills would not have seen another lighted curtain for miles.

I don't think he knocked. He probably leant on the back door and its latch at the same time, and both opened. His clothes were torn and he was plastered with dried mud. His hair was hanging over his eyes and matted with filth. Because it was fair and lank it looked all the more disheveled and pathetic, like the forelock of a dun horse which has pitched on its head in the mud and got to its feet, without dignity or sense of direction but still game.

About his eyes there was nothing at all pathetic. Within the tangle they reflected the light or, perhaps, projected it. As he rose, very wobbly, from the kitchen floor, I had the impression of a desperate string of muscles carrying about a brain which could no longer give sensible orders but wouldn't stop issuing them. He reminded me of a very busy man with a bad attack of malaria.

I shut the door and eased him into a chair. I then saw that skin as well as clothes had been ripped. He was oozing blood from long, shallow scratches; it was that rather than mud which had matted his hair. He stretched out his arm on the kitchen table and rested his head on it. When he looked up at me from that angle, his eyes were even more disturbing. I thought he muttered:

"I want a woman."

A normal enough remark in private among friends. But as an explanation to a complete stranger of one's arrival it was a danger signal. My immediate reaction was to wonder if he would stay quiet while I went over to the pub to telephone a doctor or the police. Only a journey of thirty yards which was never taken. Later on, I was often to think of that.

When he repeated himself in a higher voice, it was clear that he had actually said:

"I want my woman."

The "my" made a difference that any barman would recognize. If a customer mumbled after his second whisky "I want a woman," you would give him a likely address and get rid of him; but if he said "I want my woman," you would expect the matrimonial confidences which cartoonists insist are frequent — though in fact, due to this country's licensing hours, a barman is seldom long enough alone with one customer.

"Who has taken her?" I asked, hoping that he would reveal enough of his trouble for me to begin to decide what I ought to do.

"Nobody."

"How did you get here?"

"I don't know exactly."

"Are you sure she exists? As a person, I mean."

That was hurrying it a little, but one cannot be expected to have the patience of a psychiatrist. However, he gave to my remark a second or two of whatever he could manage in the way of connected thought.

"I think she must," he said. "If she did not, what would I have done it for?"

"Done what?"

"Run here. To you."

"But she is where you came from," I answered very positively, afraid that he might have convinced himself that she was, for example, in my bedroom.

"She is? Why do you think so?"

"You couldn't know where you did come from unless she was there," I said, entering far too boldly and irrevocably into his world of obsession. "So I don't suppose anything has happened to her."

"Happened to her? Of course it hasn't! Not to her!" he exclaimed in a voice which was suddenly shrill and clear.

The upward jerk of his head disturbed his balance

— his physical balance, I mean — and I just caught him as he toppled over onto the floor. That eased for the moment the question of what I ought to do. Some elementary first aid was urgent.

I brought him round with whisky and warm milk, which was all I had in the bungalow since I took my meals over at The Green Man. Then I helped him to undress, sponged and disinfected the scratches and put him in my bed with all the blankets I could find on top of him — a precaution though he showed no sign of shock, only of exhaustion and some inner excitement. He was thin, but sinewy as a bird's leg. I remember noticing his very openwork undervest, a complicated cat's cradle of woven string. It suggested that he had bought it through the advertisement columns of some health magazine.

I hung up his tweed suit to await next morning a clothesbrush and a sewing machine, turned out the bedroom light and returned to the kitchen to draw breath. My visitor had dropped off to sleep, and there was no urgent need to make a nuisance of myself to hardworking police and ambulance men unless he became violent. Once off the subject of his woman he showed no sign of aberration, thanking me with odd formality for my assistance and curling up like a child.

Like a child, too, he offered no further explanation of himself, handing over to me his inert body with complete trust that I would do something about it. I suppose that it was primarily this simplicity which made me feel so responsible for him. He was neither short of money nor suspiciously rich. He had a few pounds in a neat wallet. His name, marked on his clothes with such care that he was either a rather prim bachelor or had a fussy wife, was H. B. Fosworthy.

Ought I to send for a doctor? Well, there was nothing more that a doctor could do for him beyond shoving a needle into him for luck. As an ex-mining engineer I know temporary exhaustion when I see it. I would have liked to wake up Mrs. Gorm and get some eggs or whatever she had in the larder. I decided to do so if Mr. H. B. Fosworthy could not sleep. Otherwise there was no point in disturbing him till he woke up and started to demand breakfast.

I poured myself a nightcap and tried to make some sense of my lunatic or criminal or deserted husband or whatever the hell he was. I was about to unpack an air mattress and turn in on the kitchen floor when there was a confident knock on the back door. I said to myself that it was obviously the police and opened up.

The man who entered was very English and certainly not a policeman. At least I unhesitatingly assumed he wasn't, though aware that my knowledge of plain-clothes detectives was entirely drawn from TV and the cinema. He had a manner which nicely combined courtesy with the assurance that everyone else was as reasonable as himself.

"I hope you will excuse me calling so late," he said, "but I saw your light on."

That meant of course that he had either come along the cart track or down from the hills. It was a little suspicious. If he had a clear right to look for my visitor, one would have expected him to follow the road and call with his inquiries at the front of The Green Man. So I pretended to misunderstand him.

"I'm afraid the pub has shut down for the night. And they haven't any rooms anyway. Just this bungalow at the bottom of the garden."

"Oh, I didn't want a room. The fact is: I am looking for somebody. And when I saw your light I thought that perhaps I might ask."

"Man or woman?"

"A man. It's rather a sad case. He gets off by himself sometimes, and that leads to embarrassment. We don't want to put him under any restraint."

Still playing for time and hoping to avoid direct questioning, I said that I had been led to believe that mental hospitals in these days could nearly always cure.

"Well, yes," he admitted. "But when it is just extreme eccentricity, one hesitates . . . You haven't seen him then?"

"I thought I heard a noise in the stables some time back," I said, with the idea of protecting myself in case this were a genuine inquiry.

"Do you think anyone would mind if I had a look round?"

"Well, I don't. And everyone else is asleep."

"I'll do that then," he said.

"Do you want any help?"

"No, don't bother! I've disturbed you enough already. Very many thanks."

I saw the beam of a powerful electric torch thoroughly searching the deserted buildings. Curious to see where he went when he had finished, I slipped out of the bungalow's front door into the pub garden. From behind the hedge I watched him hesitate about calling on me again, then climb a gate and disappear across the fields.

It reinforced my guess that he had come that way. I wondered why he had firmly refused help, why he was looking for his eccentric friend on foot instead of proceeding by car from village to village and police station to police station. If he had arrived openly, called first at the pub and then walked across the garden to the bungalow with Gorm, I should at once and thankfully have handed over Mr. H. B. Fosworthy. As it was, I felt that morning would be soon enough for decision. The man in my bed was certainly peculiar, to put it charitably, but I now had a worrying presentiment that he was also very much afraid. I doubt if I had spotted it earlier.

I had no friends or connections locally. Not many anywhere in England, if it came to that. My practical experience as a mining engineer was extensive, but my qualifications were not. So when I made a small killing in Canadian tin — owing to the generosity of a grateful board in financing my purchase of shares — I decided to give up a profession in which I could never reach the top and to start a new life in my own country while I was still young enough to be enterprising. I intended to buy an inn and a garage, near a main road but not on it, and develop the pair together. Mine was not a high ambition, but I was confident that I could pull it off. I'm a good mechanic myself and can spot in five minutes whether an employee knows his job. As for catering and comfort, I have lived for fifteen years in camps and hotels and can smell what a customer likes and what he doesn't.

That was what had brought me to The Green Man. My agents told me it was on the market. I was having a look at the bar takings, which were not very big, the available space, which could easily be converted into eight bedrooms and baths, and the garage — which did not exist but could well be made from the coach house and stables provided one metaled the hundred yards of cart track.

Being a stranger, therefore, I had nowhere to go for advice and no judgment to rely on but my own. I would have been happier if this emergency had hit me in some camp on the edge of the tundra where one hopes for the visitor who never arrives, rather than in a tame but unfamiliar English hamlet. For the moment it seemed best to continue to lie low and say nothing. So I locked all the doors and windows and went to sleep.

There wasn't a sound out of Fosworthy. About seven I looked in on him. He was wide awake, lying on his back and watching the ceiling so intently that I followed his eyes to see if there were a mosquito or a leak or something.

He thanked me in precise language, but very warmly, and assured me that there was nothing wrong with him except that he was stiff.

"I'd better tell you at once that someone was looking for you," I said. "A close relation, I think."

"Not a relation. Dear me, no! A former colleague would be approximately correct."

"He seemed to be sure you weren't far away."

"Yes. If my impetus had not carried me halfway over the wire, he would have caught me. He even got a hand on my shoe."

"What wire?" I asked, with some vague mental image of concentration camps or Berlin walls.

"Two fields up there. On the edge of the downs."

Then I knew what he was talking about, for I had noticed the formidable hedge and heard from Mrs. Gorm why it was there.

Opinions for and against field sports ran strong and very deep in that countryside. The farmer who owned the land between The Green Man and the western slopes of the Mendips objected to fox hunting. His boundary fence reflected his determination to keep a heartless world out rather than to keep his cattle in. It was a high, double hawthorn hedge, well trimmed and ditched, with two quite unnecessary strands of barbed wire down the middle.

I could understand Fosworthy's condition on arrival. If his "impetus" had carried him into the hedge — presumably headfirst — he must have been in it for long minutes trapped and writhing while a more cautious arm felt for him. And all this when he was exhausted after a cross-country run!

"You got through it?" I asked, amazed that he wasn't still helplessly stuck.

"Yes. And then I saw your light and forced myself to run again."

The pursuer had never attempted the hedge, for his clothes were not torn. I suppose he trotted along it looking for some break. When he found that there was no way out, he retraced his steps to the upper gate or gap through which they had stumbled, followed the boundary round to the road and at last came down the cart track in search of the lighted window that he, too, had noticed.

"Look here!" I said. "Shouldn't you be having treatment of some sort?"

"I don't think so. The scratches are all very shallow, and I never suffer from infections."

I gave up that line. In any case the innuendos of the other man were probably lies. Fosworthy did not seem at all unbalanced in broad daylight.

"You're on the run? Some trouble with the police?"

"I'm a vegetarian," he said.

"What has that got to do with it?"

"Quite a lot. But it doesn't matter. I just mentioned the fact to show you that I do not take life if I can help it."

"I didn't mean I thought you were a murderer," I assured him. "I was just wondering about the law — or, well, politics."

"Nothing to do with either," he replied. "They both avoid essentials."

"For example?"

"Metaphysical animism. What is your religion?"

"Well, I put myself down on a form as Church of England."

"We are not considering the purely sectarian," he rebuked me. "You are a Christian then?"

"Naturally."

"It's not particularly natural. But it's a good start. I think I had better be going now."

Suppressing yaps of pain, he hauled himself out of the bed and sat on the edge of it.

"Where to?"

"I have to see her again. Affinity is surely undeniable. Loving her as I do, she must be ready to love me. Then we could go far away."

"Hadn't you better tell me a little more?"

"Definition is so often destructive," he replied. "It may help you to know that to myself I call her Undine."

I couldn't care less what he called her. But he produced this sentimental nonsense with so serious an air that it was up to me to show interest. So I asked why.

"She has blue veins."

"Don't we all?"

"My good sir, I was not referring to the back of your hand! I meant that her skin is so pellucid that she might, to my eyes and if I may put it so, be the nymph of an enchanted lake. That perfection is indeed the reason why I find myself in your care, for I have recently become convinced —" he looked at me as if I were an intelligent schoolboy about to be enriched by an eager master — "entirely convinced that when our bodies are ethereal we may not distinguish the extremes of physical beauty."

I replied politely that no doubt he was right.

"What do *you* believe happens to you when you dissolve?" he asked.

That was the first time I heard this word which was to become so detestable.

"Well, it's a bit difficult to know, isn't it?"

"Then if you suffer from all the absurd anxieties of mankind, I think you had better get out of here," he replied with sudden, disturbing return to everyday life. "He'll borrow a dog and be back with it this morning. The dog will track me here, but so long as this bungalow is locked up and I lay a trail, he will assume I hesitated at the door and went off again. The dog cannot tell him that I entered under your charitable roof. That insures that you will be unmolested. I fear that I have been instrumental in working my friends into a sad state of excitement in which they are quite likely to commit acts of violence that afterwards they would regret."

I told him patiently that I was a simple, uncomplicated engineer, and that at least he owed it to me to put things clearly.

"All I've got so far," I said, "is that you are frightened but that it wouldn't be important if you hadn't fallen in love with a girl one can see through."

"Though crudely objective, that is about it," he admitted.

"But forgive me if I say it seems inadequate."

"Love and death? Inadequate?"

"I'll see about getting you some breakfast," I said, giving up.

"I don't want to involve anybody else."

"You won't. I'll manage without giving your presence away."

"And how about this?" he asked, turning back the sheets. "My word, what a mess!"

In my far too hasty Good Samaritan act I had not foreseen the state of sheets and pillowcase. Or rather I had not thought it important. I never suspected that in the morning there would be any reason for secrecy. The linen was nowhere soaked, but of course spotted by far more blood than could be explained by a shaving cut.

He went into a huddle with himself, quite unembarrassed by silent thought, and at last emerged to ask me what I had done with his clothes. When I replied that they were in the cupboard, he hopped inside to have a look.

"Thank you," he said, peering round the open door like a tame crow, eyes bright with his own incomprehensible cleverness. "Would you care to give me your hand?"

"Of course."

Quick and decisive as a surgeon he drew two scores from my wrist to my knuckles with a savage twig of hawthorn which he had extracted from his coat. I damned his eyes and very nearly called him a sadistic lunatic.

"It's for your own protection. Really it is," he said with mild surprise.

My exasperated opinion was that he had an obsession with blue veins. He had neatly nicked one of mine. I asked him how the devil he thought I could explain ripping myself twice in a tidy, modern room without so much as a rusty nail in the wall.

"You found a poor little pussy crawling around with a broken back, and when you tried to put it out of pain . . ."

"I don't put poor little pussies out of pain! I get some-one else to do it."

"Then you are very muddled on the subject like many other people."

But the excuse was good, blast him! When I went over to the pub for breakfast, I used the cat on the Gorms — helping it, not putting it out of pain — and explained that the handkerchief with which I had bound up my hand had slipped while I was asleep. Mrs. Gorm said that I should have put my coat over the cat's head, and did an efficient job on me with adhesive dressings.

She believed in a good breakfast and found in me a guest after her own heart. I could hardly secrete fried eggs in my pocket, but bacon, sausages and a slice of ham were easy. Then, getting up from the table, I re-membered that Fosworthy was a vegetarian. That beat me. What did vegetarians have for breakfast? There seemed to be nothing but toast and marmalade which was safe. So I packed a pile of that in a paper napkin and surreptitiously picked half a dozen carrots and a cabbage on my way back through the garden.

When I went into the bedroom, I found that he had had a bath. He looked very different. He would have passed as, say, a devoted preparatory schoolmaster in his early forties if his clothes had not been in ribbons. He actually ate the raw carrots and much of the cab-bage, neatly shredding them with a pocket knife — proof enough, I should have thought, that human teeth were never meant for such a diet.

I watched him — stared would be a better word —

while he performed his conjuring trick of making a cabbage disappear. I could not make him out at all. He had luminous gray eyes in a thin face of yellowish tan: a complexion which may have been due as much to rabbit food as to sun. The hollow cheeks and remarkable eyes could look mild and intelligent, as now they did, or crazily energetic under stress.

"About your movements," I said. "I have finished my business here and I needn't stay any longer. I'll drive you wherever you want to go."

He hesitated over this, and repeated that it was his duty to protect me. He pointed out that he still had to lay a trail for the dog.

"Damn the dog! There isn't any dog," I exclaimed. "And unless it's trained it can't tell him anything for certain. All we have to bother about is somebody sitting in comfort on the edge of the downs with a pair of field glasses. If you really believe that is possible, I'll try to smuggle you into the car unobserved."

Since his coat was unwearable, I gave him a high-necked sweater of mine, and we pinned up the biggest of the rents in his trousers. I felt dubious whether he was in any real danger at all. Still, the fact remained that his imagination had been sufficiently stirred to dive through the solidest hedge in the country of Somerset. Presumably Undine's husband — as good a theory as another — did not believe in affinities and cabbage.

The odd thing was that the husband had not seemed in the least angry. Not out of breath. Perfect composure. Excellent manners. He could have been a soldier or a local squire. The compact body, the clothes, the close-clipped dark moustache, the ease and intimacy of address were those of a man with his roots deep in the countryside.

I paid my bill at The Green Man and drove off up the road, then turned into the cart track as if I meant to pick up my bag at the bungalow and save myself the trouble of walking across the garden with it. I told Fosworthy to leave by the front door and work his way on hands and knees round the bungalow into the shelter of the little ornamental hedge. He could then reach the garden gate, which I would leave open, and crawl through it under cover of the car without anyone seeing him except the Gorms. As they were busy cleaning up the bar and shortsighted anyway, the risk was small.

It worked. I reversed very slowly with Fosworthy crawling alongside until trees covered us from any observer in the fields or on the downs. He got in and sat on the floor.

We had traveled a mile or two towards Cheddar when he started fussing again about that improbable dog. I gave way to him and drove back until we came to a bend where there was a field gate, just out of sight of the entrance to the cart track. This was likely to be the point where the other fellow had hit the road and he might well revisit it before investigating the now empty bungalow. At any rate Fosworthy proposed to leave his scent there. I suggested derisively that he should do it on the gate post. He considered this in long silence, as if it might be an important contribution to modern philosophy, but decided to have a roll on the grass verge instead. He then discovered that he had left his coat behind in the bungalow.

I told him to stay where he was, and not for God's sake to attract the attention of passing motorists by rolling on the ground as if he were having a fit. I drove back, recovered his coat, rolled it up and chucked it into the boot of the car.

When I was approaching the junction with the road, my other visitor of the night appeared on the edge of the cart track and waved me down. He asked if I would be good enough to give him a lift. Wherever he had been, he could not have seen anything — except of course that I had forgotten some possession at the bungalow and gone back to fetch it. The dog existed only in Fosworthy's dreams.

"Have you found your friend?" I asked.

"No. It's quite hopeless. Where are you going now?"

Fosworthy was only just round the corner of the road, on the way to Cheddar; so I replied that I was going to Wells.

"That will do fine," he said, sitting down beside me.

I shot out of the cart track and made a thoroughly dangerous U-turn. For all I knew, Fosworthy might have been inspired to lay a trail by strolling after me. His reactions were incalculable.

"What have you done to your hand?" my companion asked.

He seemed to me a less sensitive type than Mrs. Gorm or myself, so I gave him the putting-out-of-pain story, saying that the noise in the stables which I had mentioned to him turned out to be an injured cat.

"I see," he said. "You should have apologized to it."

"I can't speak cat."

"Nor can I, or only a very little," he laughed. "But when you have to kill, if you calm yourself, you calm the animal. We are all the same."

There was something vaguely reminiscent of Fosworthy in that remark. Otherwise the man appeared pleasant and normal. He chatted easily of sheep farming on the Mendips and moorland reclamation, and did not tell me his name. I myself let him know that I had been a mining engineer and added: "But it's a hotel I'm after now."

I meant only to explain my innocent presence at the bungalow; but, thinking over the conversation, I can see that the little word "now" was possibly unfortunate.

When we reached Wells, he asked me to drop him at the police station. I was sufficiently interested to hang around out of sight and see what he did. As soon as he thought I had driven away, he came out of the station. He might have had time to ask at the desk whether, for example, a pair of gloves had been found, but not for any serious report or inquiry. It was a bit of evidence in favor of Fosworthy's implication that this was a very private affair — if indeed he had ever said anything so definite.

I was back at the gate where I had left him in twenty minutes altogether. He was not there, nor was he behind a hedge or in any of the ditches. He had vanished. I was not as relieved to lose him as common sense insisted I should be. He had aroused a sort of paternal and exasperated affection. Besides that, I was fasci-

nated by such individuality in a society which seemed
to me to be composed of shades of gray — pleasant
and restful enough, but lacking the color of the decidedly unwelfarish world in which I had been let loose
ever since my schooldays.

At any rate it was the society for which I was nostal-
gic, and I continued the search for my future inn. The
Green Man would nearly do, but I was in no hurry. I
hoped to find something more to my taste, preferably
on or just below the Mendips.

Why there? That question turned out to be so difficult to explain convincingly that I must dig down for
the motives which at the time of my pub-hunting were
largely unconscious and instinctive.

My mother was Welsh and spoke her language with
pride whenever she could find anyone to speak it to —
which was seldom, since we lived at Bampton on the
edge of Exmoor. My father was an agricultural engineer: in fact, a blacksmith who had moved on from
horses to tractors.

She was quietly proud of her ancestry, which
she traced back to native princes of Wales — romantically, no doubt — and it was on her stories of the West
that I was brought up. I say the West because the bardic
legends covered the whole of the Roman-Celtic nation
which so long endured on both sides of the Bristol
Channel.

How can one explain these acquisitions of childhood
which penetrate into a man as a cat's mouse-catching
lessons into her kittens? Put it this way! I had a frontier
of the imagination which corresponded to the dim but

real frontier of Ambrosius and Arthur. My own true country of choice and spirit ran from the Wansdyke to Land's End — and this though no one could have been more stolid, ruddy and Saxon than my father at his forge.

When I decided on my new profession, it was the Bristol Channel which tempted me. Devon and Cornwall were too full of holiday-makers for my taste. That may sound odd for an innkeeper, but what I wanted — as much emotionally as financially — was trade all the year round. So for me the answer was a Somerset village, not too low-lying, not too near Bristol, not on the coast. And my personal predilection — here comes in Mother again — was for the Mendips and Glastonbury. Mysterious Glastonbury, holy to the Celtic Christians and long before. Avalon, the burial place of Arthur. Ynys Witrin, the island fort of glass which guards the Underworld. In all the explanations of that tradition which I have come across, I have never seen mentioned the simplest of all: that Glastonbury does in fact guard the way to the Underworld. Beyond it, to the traveler coming up from the south, are the hollow Mendips, the silence of death and the unknown waters of the caves.

It was the morning of September 3 when Fosworthy vanished from the roadside. Some ten days later I was staying at Taunton for the weekend. In the hotel lounge I got into conversation with a man of about my own age, evidently somewhat bored and tired but scientifically restoring his spirits by carefully timed measures of vodka. He was dryly amusing and very informative.

He lived in a village between Wells and Glastonbury and was a consulting psychiatrist.

As so often happens, he was interested by my mining shop, and I by his account of incredible brain experiments going on in Bristol. We decided to share a table at dinner. Dr. Dunton then suggested that he had a much better idea for my lonely evening than a movie, and asked me to come along as his guest to a big annual dance at the county mental hospital. When I foolishly hesitated, he said that it would educate me, that I ought to see how the other half lived, and so on.

"This dance does the influential public the hell of a lot of good and doesn't do the patients any harm," he added. "There's no alcohol served, of course, but you can always slip out to the car park where some of us will be delighted to keep you cheerful. That's why I am staying the night."

It did not seem too bad a prospect, especially since I was already in an expansive mood.

"By the way, do you know if they ever had a local patient called Fosworthy?" I asked.

"They didn't," he replied. "But I sometimes think they ought to have, if you mean our H. Barnabas Fosworthy. How did you run across him?"

The whole episode, at that distance and after dinner, appeared humorous and unlikely; but his question sobered me up instantly. I wished I had never mentioned Fosworthy. He had been so insistent that it might be unhealthy for me to be connected with him. And, after all, there was some evidence that I should be stupid not to fall in with his wishes.

"It was just that he wrote me a crazy letter about the origin of tin."

"Yes, some daft geological theory would be right up his street," said Dunton. "His chief interest is in primitive religion. All from books, of course!"

"What does he do?"

"Nothing. A bachelor, living on a reasonable income of his own. He's a funny fellow, much liked and much laughed at. When he first came here, he was always agitating against taking life. But then, very oddly, some of the sporting set began to consider him a sort of local prophet, though they didn't give up their fun. Our countryside is full of the intelligent half-educated."

"It should just about suit me then," I said.

"Oh, I didn't mean chaps from wide, open spaces! It's the effect of Glastonbury I'm talking about. There's such a climate of myth and death about the place. Jung and his collective unconscious is a much safer guide than Freud around here, but don't tell anyone I said so!"

We took a taxi over to the county hospital. There were rows of expensive cars outside. Inside, the hall was banked with flowers and gaily decored. Dunton introduced me to a number of doctors and nurses — many of them foreigners who decidedly knew how to dress for the occasion. It was impossible to distinguish visitors from patients. Well, of course it was. I couldn't imagine why I should have expected straws in the hair.

I danced a bit, for there was an excellent band, and then visited the car park where I was pressed to choose between champagne in a car belonging to a visiting psychiatrist from the Midlands, and Dunton's bottle of brandy. It was becoming a really outstanding occasion. I hoped that the following year my new hotel would be able to lay on a special dinner beforehand.

I returned to the hall with Dunton, the registrar and the prosperous headshrinker. While we stood watching the floor, my eye was caught by the lovely slim figure of a girl in a gold-and-white evening frock who was dancing a waltz — the more frenzied modern minuets were carefully avoided — with grace and abandon. When her partner brought her round to us, I was still more interested. She had a small head, with very definite but delicate features. set on a long neck. She was, I recognized, what a river nymph ought to look like, cold, exquisite, of tremulous and uncertain boundaries. One had to examine her closely to see why. Her skin was indeed as transparent as water, and the capillaries showed as a blue mist. At that first sight of her I could not decide whether she fascinated me or not. I never could. I always remained an interested neutral. The effect of that marvelous complexion depended on the light. She could appear slightly grotesque or appealingly and tragically fragile.

"Is that a patient or a guest?" I asked.

"A guest," said the registrar. "She lives in Bath, I believe. Do you want to meet her?"

"Not much. She's too untouchable."

Since her frock revealed a good half of delightful high breasts, that was an odd adjective; but I well remember using it. I suppose that instinct really does have some validity in the field of sexual attraction.

"Myself I find blue willow pattern more attractive to

eat off," Dunton remarked callously. "Still, I can imagine the excitement of following the design wherever it led you."

"Oh, God! Excuse me!" the registrar exclaimed.

A harmless-looking gray-haired chap, whom I would have put down as a male nurse, had just barged his way onto the dance floor and dropped on his knees before her, babbling. She seemed accustomed to it, or else she was wonderfully tactful by nature. She continued to smile at the poor devil without a trace of embarrassment until he was unobtrusively led away.

The registrar returned to us, a good deal more troubled than she had been.

"That hardly ever happens," he assured us. "A charming patient, too! A quite brilliant paranoiac who spends all his time working out the mathematics of a flat, circular universe!"

Dunton's mind was still on the girl. He wondered whether she lacked a layer of epidermis or had little skin pigmentation. He said she would have to be damned careful to keep out of the sun.

"The sun!" exclaimed the Midlands psychiatrist. "What the devil has a woman like that to do with sun and beaches and vulgarity? God! Just think of her naked in candlelight!"

He cleared his throat loudly and medically to cover up his most undisciplined comment. I was somewhat shocked. But, after all, I suppose psychiatrists have to let their hair down sometimes like the rest of us. And I suspected that Fosworthy's one remaining thought when he arrived exhausted at the bungalow might have been much the same. There could not be two such women.

I was too uneasy to enjoy the rest of the party, for it struck me that where one of Fosworthy's perturbations was, the other might well turn up. In that case I could imagine Dunton introducing me and cheerfully mentioning before I could stop him that I knew Barnabas Fosworthy. Nor did I want to slip away, since something similar might happen in my absence and I should never know about it. Misgivings were not farfetched. My mysterious visitor with the moustache was the type one would be sure to meet at any social function of importance to the county. I was certain that he was not mysterious to anyone but me.

I was therefore very ready to go when the Midlands mindhealer offered us a lift back to the hotel. He seemed rather glum and disappointed in spite of some pretty affectionate dancing with Fosworthy's Undine. Dunton, however, was inclined to sing madrigals. At breakfast next morning I found him just as pleasant with a headache as without one. He insisted that I should call on him if I were anywhere near his village in the evening after a day's pub-hunting. I promised to do so.

The Taunton district had not produced anything I liked. The Green Man was still at the top of my list. Before returning to London, I dropped in to check some details of the existing plumbing. Mr. Gorm said he had a telephone message for me which he had been hanging onto in case I turned up. He hunted about for the slip of paper and found it among bottles behind the bar.

*If I sees Mr. Yarrow, would he be so very kind as to call
on Mr. Smith at 34 Petunia Avenue, Hammersmith.*

I did not know a Mr. Smith who could conceivably
want to see me. Was there a mistake in the name? No,
Gorm said, the caller had not known my name. He had
just asked for the gentleman who had been staying in
the bungalow.

"So very kind as to" — that was Fosworthy all right.
Added proof was that I had never had the time or the
occasion to introduce myself. I was relieved to hear that
he was all in one piece, though persuading himself that
it was necessary to take refuge in the wilds of Hammersmith under an alias. I had felt guilty — when I
thought about it at all — at having let him down
through no fault of my own.

The following afternoon I drove out to Hammersmith. Thirty-four Petunia Avenue was a small boardinghouse, self-consciously bright, with a ROOM AND
BREAKFAST notice in the window. The proprietress answered the bell herself, and I asked for Mr. Smith.

"Oh, we are so glad that somebody has called to see
him," she cried. "He hardly ever goes out, you know,
and we were getting a little worried about him."

I assured her that there was nothing to worry about,
that when Mr. Smith was not in London he lived all
alone in the country and perhaps had got set in his
ways.

I knocked on his door. When he opened it, his face lit
up with relief and gratitude. I cannot think of a time
when anyone seemed so pleased to see me. It reinforced
my affection for him.

He was no longer agitated. In fact he looked very quiet and miserable. He was thinner than ever, and his cheeks alarmingly hollow. I said I was afraid he had been allowing his imagination to get out of hand.

"Bless me, no!" he replied. "But I have had nothing much to eat since I last saw you. I had just enough to pay for my first week here, and then no money at all."

I reckoned — having been flat broke in my time — that I could have carried on for a couple of weeks on boardinghouse breakfasts without showing signs of starvation; but then I remembered his diet.

"They are most obliging in falling in with my wishes," he told me. "They give me two dainty rolls and a plate of lettuce every morning, but of course it is not enough."

I offered to go out at once and buy some nut cutlets or whatever he fancied, if he knew of a shop in the neighborhood where I could get them.

"I cannot understand why it should be thought that there is something recondite about vegetarianism," he said with a flash of spirit. "A brown loaf and a pot of honey would do excellently."

"And some milk?"

"I have an aversion to London milk. Or, to be fair, the small jug I am given with my breakfast is somewhat tasteless. A bottle of stout — if I might trespass so far upon your astonishing kindness."

I was back in ten minutes with his order. He got outside the whole loaf and three-quarters of a pound of honey. Then he put down a pint of stout with hearty enjoyment. If anyone had asked me, I should have replied automatically that vegetarians did not touch alcohol — probably with some vague thought of pious Hindus.

I was so occupied by the situation in which he had managed to land himself that only now did I have a chance to tell him what had happened when I drove back to the bungalow to recover his coat.

"I guessed something of the sort," he said, "and ventured to beg a lift from a passing truck which took me to Reading. I must admit I find hitchhiking, as I believe it is called, an unwarranted intrusion upon strangers, but they do not seem to mind. From Reading I walked most of the way to Hammersmith and took this room. Then my circumstances became almost desperate, so I risked that telephone call. There was no one else to help and advise me.

"But don't you have friends in London?" I asked.

"Very few. And they would not understand."

I could not see why he was short of cash. I explained — trying not to be patronizing — that he could draw a check or transfer money to an account in Hammersmith.

"I should have to give an address," he said, "and I cannot trust my bank manager not to reveal it. Since I vanished from home without warning, there could be quite innocent inquiries about me apart from the others."

"Does this bank manager know your investments?"

"Yes, of course. I am afraid my life is an open book."

That was a remarkable statement, if there ever was one.

"But if you really are in danger, why don't you go to the police?"

"It would involve so much. And I could not be a traitor merely because of disagreement with my associates."

This was utterly sincere: an essential part of his simplicity. I replied that the person or persons from whom he was hiding seemed to be poor judges of character.

"I am bad at explaining. I get too emotional, you see. I can understand that they mistrust me and are very anxious to insure my silence. I am in love and cannot help it. I fear I run into strange capers, as Shakespeare said."

"I seem to remember that you want to run away with her."

"To be with her."

"How many times have you met this girl of yours?"

"Twice."

If it had just been Fosworthy and the higher mathematician, I should have decided that Undine had a pathological effect on confirmed bachelors in their early forties. But I also remembered the reaction of the psychiatrist. At first sight of her he had sounded ready to leave home, family and profession. And there were Dr. Dunton and I, the one finding her as unattractive as if she were painted with woad, and the other merely curious!

"And that's enough to convince you that some secret or other is worthless?" I asked.

"I see you have a gift for distinguishing essentials, my dear Yarrow! An individual cannot be destroyed. Therefore dissolution is a mere inconvenience, though frightening if there is no preparation or apology. But since I have come to know perfection, the life of the flesh appears to me to be of greater value than I suspected. I may have mentioned my doubt that blue veins carry on into the next world."

"So long as you believe you see them, it doesn't seem to me to matter very much," I said.

He retorted that solipsism — which seemed to be a textbook term for what I had said — was the resort of the intellectually lazy, and continued to lecture me. As soon as he gave me a chance by drawing breath for the next paragraph, I returned to his practical problems and offered a simple solution.

"You open an account in Hammersmith or where you wish. I guarantee the initial overdraft, putting up some cover if the manager wants it. Then you write to the companies whose shares you hold, instructing them to send your dividends to the bank. I don't see how that can go wrong. It gives you a breather before anyone can trace you."

"You would really do this for me?" he asked.

"Well, I don't mind. And meanwhile I'll pay your bill for the last week and calm down the landlady."

His private income, he told me, was around £2,000 a year. On that he kept up a considerable library, a comfortable cottage and a cook-housekeeper who came in every morning, served lunch, left his supper in the larder and cleared off home. He had written to her from Reading that he had been called away. He hoped that would prevent her getting anxious about him.

It was about time he sweetened his housekeeper again, so I offered to post, at the other end of London, a cheerful card from him.

"When you fell into the bungalow that night, how long had you been on the run?" I asked.

"Not long. Since about eight o'clock."

"Good Lord! I thought it was days."

"I never had much of a lead, you see."

"You mean, you just kept running with the other chap close behind?"

"Yes. There was no time to hide or think or anything."

"But since eight!" I exclaimed. "It isn't dark till nine. You must have passed people and houses and you must have crossed roads, both of you running like hell. That's hardly credible!"

"I cannot explain any more," he said formally, with the old-fashioned little bow he used. "I ask you to accept that, until well after dark, we were in a place where there were no strangers."

"That reminds me. I still have your coat in the car. I'll fetch it before I forget."

One chucks things into the boot and then ceases to notice them. I was sure that his coat was there along with an old windbreaker, a bit of ground sheet for kneeling on, some oily rags and a torn seat cover. I turned the whole lot out twice. The coat was not there.

I did not mention it to him for fear of arousing all sorts of fantasies which would merely muddle me. I just said that the coat, after all, must be in my flat.

But I knew it wasn't. My misgivings returned. What about that dance where I had reasonably feared that the dark-moustached country gentleman might turn up? Possibly he had — and then it would have been easy for him to find out how Dunton and I had arrived and where we were staying the night. Plenty of time for a quick examination of my car in the hotel garage. It may not have been locked. The boot certainly was not.

I could not tell how far Fosworthy imagined dogs and dangers, nor make any sense of Undine's connection with metaphysical animism, whatever that was. It was clear, however, that the man who had chased him to my door now knew that I had taken him in; so it would be assumed that I had asked for explanations, found them of interest to me and concealed his presence — deliberately and for some good reason concealed his presence. We all expect other people to have rational motives, though we know very well that our own acts are half of them due to impulse.

A couple of days later I took Fosworthy along to the bank where I had fixed up the account. He looked very much better. I never knew a man to recover so quickly from strain or worry. The next time I called to see him he had gone, leaving no address. Not out of my life. I was sure of that. Sooner or later there would be an appeal to sign his girl's passport application or some other top-secret absurdity. Address: The Meads. Parents' nationality: Extramundane. Hair: Long. To hell with it!

I was uneasy about my connection with him and his affairs but not at all alarmed. If I did some day have to answer police or private inquiries as to what I thought I was up to, my straight explanation would be that I liked him, that I believed I had rescued him and that I felt obscurely responsible. I attached no importance whatever to the mystery which he was suspected of betraying. As likely as not, it would turn out to be a Fairy Flag made in Birmingham or a fake Roman bowl which he and his friends had decided was the Holy Grail. On a miniature scale that corner of Somerset was as flush as Southern California with little nests and covens of earnest believers in almost anything.

Shortly afterwards my agents sent me particulars — which were completely misleading — of an inn at Axbridge. One look at it from the outside was enough. So I had a free afternoon on my hands with the weather set fine.

Lunching meditatively alone, I considered Fosworthy's possible movements. He had been on the run from eight, but, if I understood him, had only taken to the open when it was night — say, about ten. Then the place he started from "where there were no strangers" could not be more than twelve miles from The Green Man. Half that was a more likely distance, for he must have been dodging about and changing direction according to the obstacles he came across. Thus his probable starting point was somewhere on the top of the Mendips above Westbury.

I drove up through the Cheddar Gorge — which struck me as being the most coarse and shameless commercialization of natural beauty in these islands — and then east across the plateau. I knew the roads well already. There were three big, lonely inns, none of them, unfortunately, on the market, and otherwise nothing but large, windswept farms. It was sparsely inhabited country, but the roads were never far from each other and there was a fair sprinkling of traffic. Fosworthy could easily have found or summoned help in daylight.

For close exploration one needed to be on foot or on a horse. However, I drove idly back and forth across the likely area, searching for a hint of what could have happened. Twice I saw a man on a big gray gelding at some distance from me. When I stopped at a crossroads with an extensive view and was leaning on a dry-stone wall studying the one-inch Ordnance Map, he cantered up to me.

"Are you trying to find anyone in particular?" he asked.

I hesitated and very probably looked guilty. I ought to have come out boldly with the name of a farm.

"Not exactly," I replied. "I was just thinking that if three inns could make money tucked away up here, there might be room for a fourth."

"You wouldn't stand a hope of getting a building license," he said.

"No, I'm sure I shouldn't. But it does no harm to speculate."

The word annoyed him.

"You people don't care what you do to us all so long as you can make money."

The remark was half suspicious, half contemptuous.

It was also unjust, for if I had ever had a passion for money I could have made plenty of it. I should have liked to mention some of the things which he and his fellow farmers were doing to the country for money. But I saw no point in arguing, so I nodded a good afternoon and cleared off.

As I drove down into Wells, I remembered that Dr. Dunton lived only a couple of miles on, along the Glastonbury road, and decided to call on him. It was well after six, so he ought to be home from his consulting room.

His eighteenth-century house was immaculate and very satisfying to the eye. Around it was an area of hospitable untidiness. A generously built woman with splendid eyes was washing a dog on the front steps. Four ponies in various stages of undress were being attended by four girls between seven and thirteen. An older boy lay on an uncut lawn, listening to pops on a transistor set and detaching himself pointedly from the feminine obsession with animals.

I introduced myself and apologized for so casual a visit. Mrs. Dunton couldn't care less. I felt that she loved any newcomer so long as he or she could take the family as it was. Dunton had kept his private life completely separate from his profession and avoided any nonsense of competing with the Joneses. I suppose that if he had practiced at home he could not have lived in so delightfully free and easy a way.

"He told me about you," Mrs. Dunton said. "He's round the back somewhere. Pat will show you. And supper is at seven and of course you'll stay for it."

Pat, with a pair of plaits which were gloriously clean and golden and a pair of jodhpurs crusted with mud and horsehair, led me round the house and handed me over to her father. He was in a deck chair, a tray of drinks and a book at his side, and he greeted me, like the rest of them, as if I were his next-door neighbor. I told him where I had been in the course of the day, and after a drink and some casual conversation asked:

"Do you remember saying that this country was full of the intelligent half-educated?"

"I don't. But after dinner it's quite likely."

"Have you ever run across the idea of apologizing to anything you kill before you kill it?"

"I'm a psychiatrist, not a surgeon," he said.

Vaguely and incompetently I tried to explain what I meant.

"Now, which of these coons have you been talking to?" he asked. "Aviston-Tresco?"

"Who's he?"

"Our most fashionable vet. And a damned good one."

"What does he look like?"

"Very much the country gentleman. Well dressed, compact, with a short, dark moustache. I'd put him down as a major in a cavalry regiment, if there were any cavalry regiments."

"Has he anything to do with the transparent woman?"

"Not so far as I know. But I tell you who is a close friend of his — that queer fish Barnabas Fosworthy who gave you his unasked opinion on the origin of tin."

"Is there anyone among your vet's associates who

[38]

farms on the top of the Mendips and rides a big gray gelding?"

"Yes. Why?"

"Nothing. He was keeping me under observation this afternoon, and at last rode up to see what I was doing. I mentioned sites for pubs."

Dunton began to interrogate me in the pleasantest possible way. Where had I been looking for my inns, and since when? What places had I inspected? I answered with a frankness which must have convinced him of my sincerity; but he was a modest man and distrusted his own judgment.

"I'm going to be indiscreet," he said at last. "Isn't your pub-hunting cover for something else?"

"Good God, no! Why do you think so?"

"Because you have asked a number of connected questions."

"Just curiosity," I replied — which was true enough so far as it went. "An innkeeper is like a priest. He wants to know all about the parish before he accepts the living."

"Neat!" he smiled. "But if you ever feel like telling me all the truth, remember that psychiatrists keep just as many secrets as landlords and priests."

This was too good a chance to miss. I told him that an impulsive act of mine, which seemed charitable at the time, had involved me with a bunch of believers in something odd, and I wanted to know what they did believe.

"I've had a patient among them and got some of it out of her," he said. "All life is one and interchanges communication. Death is a mere break in continuity, but it may be momentarily inconvenient or painful. So, if you hand it out, you should express regret. That somehow creates unity with the victim and wipes the slate clean. My patient was obsessed by hunting. In her Rorschach tests she saw antlers, tusks, foxes, heads of imaginary animals. Always death and relics of death.

"Well, such a creed is attractive to anyone who loves killing birds and beasts. It has some affinity to the sorrow which big-game hunters tell us they feel when they have destroyed a very fine animal. I feel it myself when my daughters send for me to squash a large, very perceptive spider. There's a moment of fellowship with the creature. The funny thing is that this belief is also a comfort to people who hate killing — like this Fosworthy who won't and Tom Aviston-Tresco who has to."

"You mean that if one were shooting pheasants," I asked incredulously, "it would be just: Bang, bang! 'Sorry, sorry!'?"

"I don't know that they would go so far as that." He laughed. "But I think it potentially dangerous to have no normal respect for death; so I wondered if you were not investigating officially."

I assured him again that I was not.

"Anyway it's all nonsense," Dunton went on. "This life is exciting, varied and to some lucky people beautiful, and we psychologists make it seem a lot more difficult than it is. As to the next life — if it exists — we don't know a damned thing about it. Have you ever read Teilhard de Chardin?"

"I'm afraid I haven't heard of him."

"Well, as a Jesuit he was surer of immortality than you or I can be. But the main purpose of life, he thought, was to love, enjoy and seek knowledge. And if a man gave it all he'd got he couldn't go very far wrong."

"So if one of these people fell crazily and romantically in love, it might show up his continuity stuff as a bit doubtful?"

"At any rate he would find it hard to accept death as a mere momentary inconvenience when it parted him from what he loved," Dunton answered.

That very simply explained Fosworthy for me, though not why his friends should have taken his backsliding so hard.

"The trouble is that most of them are unmarried or without children and basically lonely," Dunton added. "Suppose I hadn't the luck to have all this bouncing, exasperating, dear life around me, then I might sublimate the death wish in dozens of odd ways. But that doesn't explain the attraction of this nonsense for Tom Aviston-Tresco, who has led a most satisfying, full life ever since his wife ran away from him. I suppose that all the killing he must do has given him a neurosis, and he forgets all his healing."

The Duntons were going into Glastonbury to see a traveling circus and pressed me very warmly to join them, but I did not want to outstay my welcome. I shared their quick meal and pretended that I had business at The Green Man and had reserved a room there.

As soon as I was on the road, I decided that I might as well stay at the inn anyway instead of pointlessly dashing back to London. Although the Gorms did not normally take guests, they were happy to see that the prospective purchaser was still on the hook. And indeed I was. I often daydream of The Green Man and find myself drawing on the back of an envelope the alterations which I would have made.

About nine o'clock the man I had seen on the gray gelding came into the bar. He recognized me, handsomely asked me to forgive his rudeness in the afternoon and insisted on buying me a drink. He took a polite interest in my plans — patronizing, but not more so than was acceptable from someone who knew every inch of his country — and asked me why I particularly wanted the Mendips. I told him that I wished to avoid both the sprawling suburbs of Bristol and the coast. As I have said, I am clumsy at explaining intuitive reasons. I may have sounded as if I were almost contemptuously sparring with him.

"These hills must once have been a kind of sprawl themselves," he said.

I saw what he meant. One was seldom out of sight of the settlements and cemeteries of Neolithic and Bronze Ages breaking the smooth continuity of the grass.

I wondered how their ships got there, and ordered another round of drinks.

"Up the Bristol Channel with the prevailing southwesterlies behind them," he replied, "but a lot of them must have come to grief on Hartland. It was easier when men could simply walk from France, following the game."

"Not much of a sprawl then," I said for something to

say. "Just a skin tent here and there on the Glassy Hill."

"I believe the pundits won't have Glassy Hill any more," he remarked. "Glastonbury means the town of Glasteing."

"Then why is it called Ynys Witrin in British?"

"I didn't know it was. What does it mean?"

"The Island of Glass. And all the legends insist that it was a hill as well. It marked the way to the world underground."

"To wealth, too?" he asked, looking straight at me with a sort of challenge which I could not then understand.

"Not unless you obeyed the conditions. Like Orpheus and so forth."

"Where do you get all this from?"

"Out of the collective unconscious," I replied, trying a bit of Dunton on him.

I describe this pointless conversation because it was plain to me later why he had introduced the subject of early inhabitants. However, collective unconscious shut him up, possibly because he did not know what I was talking about — nor did I — but more probably because he did know and shied away from the term.

Very gradually he changed the subject to the question of my future hotel.

"I think I can give you a good tip," he said, "which will make up for being short with you this afternoon. If you were to call on the manager of the Somerset and Dorset Bank in Glastonbury, he could put you in touch with someone who is thinking of selling. The inn is not on the market yet."

Soon afterwards he left. When the bar closed, I asked Gorm who he was.

"Mr. Alan Jedder," he replied. "Farms five hundred acres up top. You can see his place from Twelve Barrows."

I had been nowhere near the Twelve Barrows when he rode up to me; but earlier in the afternoon I had been prying about among the tracks and earthworks of his country. So I was right in my guess. He had been keeping me under observation.

"Does he come here often?"

"Haven't seen him for donkey's years."

Gorm did not know a lot about him except that he was a bachelor, had served in the Navy and belonged to one of the wealthy families of Bristol industrialists.

The bank Jedder had mentioned was Fosworthy's. I doubted if the manager had any pub to offer me. The intention was to feel for my financial resources. Since Fosworthy was not dead — the postcards to his housekeeper proved that — he must have found somebody to lend him money.

When I had gone to bed, questions began to answer themselves. How had Jedder known where to find me? Well, he could have telephoned Aviston-Tresco, who told him to try The Green Man on the off chance that I might be there. How had he known in the afternoon that I was the man with whom Fosworthy might have shared his secret? Car number, probably.

Till then I had done no thinking about the missing coat, content to be vaguely aware that there was something illogical about it. Of course! The answer struggled up into consciousness and competed with sleep. The coat ought not to have been taken away. In that case I should never had had reason to suspect that my connection with Fosworthy was known. Then why wasn't it left in the boot? Possible answer: because I could produce it in a court of law. If that was correct, Fosworthy had really been in danger. As a corollary — whatever danger threatened him now threatened me.

In the morning I decided to visit the bank and play it their way. It would be suspicious if I took no action on a hot tip from a knowledgeable acquaintance; also I wanted to get to the bottom of the business. There was a smell of panic in all these hasty arrangements of theirs.

I allowed time for Jedder to telephone — in case he had not got in touch with the manager overnight — and turned up at the bank at midday. I was shown into the manager's office at once. My first impression was of a wispy, pepper-and-salt man with pop eyes. They were as prominent as Persian eyes, but a watery blue instead of deep brown. He was fussily dressed for the manager of a small provincial branch and already in his early fifties, which suggested that his ability was not very marked. A more charitable judgment would be that he enjoyed country life and had no ambition. Like myself, in fact. Still, I could not help feeling that he was vague and ineffective.

With a wet cordiality he discoursed on hotel finance in general and asked me what district I preferred. He knew damned well what district I preferred. I answered curtly that I wanted Glastonbury and the Mendips.

"If you should change your mind, there will shortly

be an executor's sale of a very profitable free house the other side of Bath," he said.

That was a long way from his area, so I asked him how he knew about the sale and how sure he was of it.

He was embarrassed and murmured a lot of verbiage, meant to be imposing, on the subject of the grapevine between managers. When I pressed him for details of his profitable free house, I was surer than ever that it was a clumsy invention to find out whether I should be tempted and what my resources were. I fear I was deliberately cruel to him as he wriggled in his chair and fiddled with papers.

Dropping his vague proposal as soon as he reasonably could, he told me he knew of a building site near Wookey. A license had recently fallen in and he believed that the local Bench would transfer it to a respectable hotel proprietor.

"The site belongs to a Mr. H. B. Fosworthy," he said, his pale forehead beginning to glisten with sweat. "Perhaps you know him?"

"I do not," I replied. "But I remember the name. Hadn't he escaped from a private nursing home or something?"

And I told him how a complete stranger had called at night when I was staying at The Green Man and asked me if I had seen his patient.

I thought that would fix him, and it did. He was out of his depth, uncomfortably dominated by me, and looked as if he would like to creep under his desk. I was exasperated by the silly little man, and left the bank snorting at the incompetence of these anti-Fosworthi-ans. It was only when I had driven halfway back to London that I remembered that Aviston-Tresco had never asked for Fosworthy by name. If he, too, remembered that he hadn't, I had given myself away. I thoroughly deserved it for bullying instead of meekly listening.

Three days passed — of a dullness that only an exile in London can know. You go to a show or two. You eat in restaurants. You try to get in touch with old friends who are always out or abroad or ask you to lunch the following week. You are eager to talk to anyone who will talk to you.

I had more or less dismissed Fosworthy and his affairs from my mind, deciding that all this agitation was to be expected from a bunch of religious nuts. It was possible that mysterious Avalon or the inexplicable holiness of Glastonbury might have something to do with it, but my best theory was that they had discovered uranium in the old Roman lead mines of the Mendips, that they were too impractical — including the bank manager — to have the faintest notion what to do and that muddled pacifist convictions compelled them to keep quiet. It was an improbable guess, since the hills must have been thoroughly and semi-officially prospected during the uranium boom, but it did account for the facts. They were afraid of me as a mining engineer, not as a future innkeeper.

On the fourth evening I left my depressing furnished flat to go out and buy myself a lonely meal. While I was strolling to the bus stop, I came face to face with Avis, ton-Tresco. He hailed me very cordially as if I had been an old friend. His manner did not seem forced. The strange circumstances of our previous meetings naturally created a sort of intimacy. We did not — officially — know each other's names. So he introduced himself, and so did I.

I guessed of course that his appearance in my district was no accident, but I was in a mood to hear what he had to say. Whatever his quarrel with Fosworthy, he was presentable and intelligent. Dunton had described him as brilliant in his profession and leading a full life. I think I had the idea of getting the truth out of him as one reasonable and discreet man to another. He gave me the impression that he, too, was very ready to talk.

"Would you care to come along to my club and have a drink?" he invited.

I accepted gladly. He told me that his van was parked in the next street, and we walked to it. I thought it odd that he did not use a car to come up to town, but supposed that he had bought some heavy article and was taking it home. He got in first and opened the near door. A whiff of disinfectants, straw and sheep came out. I sat down on a worn, comfortable bucket seat and was painfully pricked by a broken spring or a sliver of metal.

At my exclamation Aviston-Tresco turned round, looked me straight in the eyes with most kindly expression — not at all the spontaneous consternation that one would expect — and said:

"I am so sorry this had to happen."

Right or wrong, memory of the apology instantly

connected me to the emergency station. I leaped out of that van and ran round a couple of corners, vanishing into a nearby public lavatory which I had several times found useful. It seemed very unlikely that a really damaging quantity of any drug could be injected by a casual, deep puncture, but a culture of God-knows-what-nastiness could. I vividly remembered two cases of fulminating blood poisoning in a rain-forest camp, caused by mere scratches. Shutting the door behind me, I pulled out my pocketknife and cut a gash two inches long and half an inch deep across the point of entry — which, since there was no mirror, I could only distinguish by touch.

A broken spring. No doubt there was one. And no doubt some other sharpness, now removed, had been ingeniously attached to it. Whatever was intended to happen to me as a result of sitting down heavily and incautiously in a vet's working van would have been accepted by me and everyone else as a regrettable accident.

It wasn't going to happen to me if I could possibly help it. I shot out of the lavatory, waved down a passing car and asked to be taken to the nearest doctor. I probably looked pale and I certainly looked agitated. The long-haired young fellow who was driving did not hesitate. He was not the sort of person who refuses to be involved in unpleasantness. It's conceivable that his own activities were not always legal. At any rate he was a fortunate choice.

I tried to keep my backside well away from him, but he noticed the stain spreading on my trouser leg.

"Sit on that, cock!" he said, folding up a bit of waste. "We'll be there in five minutes. Not to worry!"

He drove me fast into the shabbier part of Westbourne Grove and rang a doctor's bell. As soon as the door opened, he cleared off discreetly with a cheerful wave.

The doctor was a youngish man and none too cordial. He was, I think, in the middle of his dinner and his surgery was closed. However, he opened the place up promptly enough when he realized that I was in need of first aid, and I was glad to see that it appeared the last word in hygiene and equipment.

"This is very urgent," I told him. "I want you to treat me as if I were in danger of anthrax or any other plague you can think of common to animals and men."

"Let me mix you a little something first," he said.

I snapped at him that I did not need a tranquilizer and was perfectly sane.

"Imagine I'm a wounded gangster," I said, "and hurry!"

I pulled down my pants, increasing his alarm, and showed him what I had done to myself.

"I ripped that open with a pocketknife. It ought to prove to you that I believe the risk to be serious. I want deep disinfecting and whatever antibiotic you think I should have."

"We can probably get along with antitetanus to start with," he said, still doubting me.

"Don't need it! I'm a mining engineer and up-to-date with my injections. You say it, I've had it."

"How about bubonic plague?" he asked with a half-smile — to find out, I think, whether my reaction would be hysterical or not.

"It could be. But if it was I should think it's washed out. I made that gash within two minutes of the puncture."

He had me face downwards on the operating table at once.

"Girls on the Underground and so forth," he said. "I've heard of such things. But the damage one can do without a syringe is pretty limited if dealt with immediately. And you did, and I'm going to. This will hurt."

He was right. And the slow injection he gave me afterwards felt like half a pint of liquid.

When I was reclining on side and elbow, very shaky but "comfortable" as they call it, he said: "I gather you think this was attempted murder. Shall I call the police for you?"

I gave it some consideration. I could not offer the police any motive or any proof that the prick was not an accident. Aviston-Tresco, a respectable, much-esteemed professional man, could show me up as panicking like a hen just because he might once have seemed a little sinister when he called on me in the middle of the night. As for the seat spring or nail or whatever it was, I had no doubt that it was still innocently projecting and that inspection would reveal nothing whatever on its tip.

"I can't prove a thing," I said.

"You mentioned diseases common to animals and

man. I think that between us we have avoided any risk of anthrax and psittacosis. But hadn't you better have a course of injections for rabies?"

I replied that I did not believe there was a chance of it. For one thing, an English vet would never have seen a case; for another, there would be headlines, inquiries and quarantines all over the country. And what was the use of giving me a disease which would appear three weeks later?

Assuming that I had not imagined the whole thing, Aviston-Tresco wanted me out of the way because he was at last dead sure that I had learned something I shouldn't from Fosworthy. Speed was therefore essential. Within a few days anthrax — a wild guess — or some virulent form of septicemia — more likely — would get me down and finish me promptly. If I never suspected that he had tried to kill me, he could sit tight. If I did come to suspect the car seat and did from my hospital bed accuse him, he was still safe. He could quite openly accept the babblings of high fever with horror and even admit that his far-from-sterile van might be responsible.

Having stitched up and plastered my backside, this now most friendly young doctor told me to come back for more injections the following day. That turned out to be impossible, and for some time I could only hope that his ministrations had done the trick. Although I was very fully occupied, there were slack hours when imagination was inclined to get out of hand and I would wonder what my temperature was.

I had something to eat — standing up — took a taxi home and limped up the stairs to my first-floor flat, asking myself why I had been so blasted courageous or cowardly in dealing with a scratch. And there, sitting on the steps which led up to the next landing, was Barnabas Fosworthy peacefully reading a book.

He shut it, got up and almost embraced me. With his shy smile, always more effective in inspiring affection than confidence, he whispered mysteriously: "I have not been followed."

I made no comment on that. He wouldn't have known it if half Somerset had trailed him up the street. I let him in and locked the door.

"I fear you have done yourself a mischief," he said.

I replied that it was just a painful touch of sciatica — for there was no point yet in telling him what had happened — and asked where he had been since he vanished from Hammersmith.

"Bristol," he answered. "I came to impart to you that, though remaining in concealment, I have been able to press my suit. I knew you would be so delighted."

Incredible! I resisted the impulse to point out that the tweed he always wore would not hold a crease.

"It was received?"

"With courtesy and a charming reserve."

"Splendid!"

"And I shall need your help."

No doubt he took my broad grin as sympathetic. Actually I had been struck by vague echoes of Bertie Wooster.

"In what way?"

"I wondered if you knew a woman of the utmost respectability."

"Possibly," I replied. "But I might be wrong. Why?"

"Miss Cynthia Carlis has appeared at my hotel. A chaperone is essential. I should not wish a breath of suspicion to rest upon her."

"But, for God's sake, you can have separate rooms!" I exclaimed. "And what makes you think she wants one anyway?"

I received the full broadside of an outraged Fosworthy. My remark was an insult to her. She was the very flower of innocent purity. One had only to look at her. How dared I?

I apologized. I begged him to believe that my view of womanhood had been corrupted by mining camps. A preposterous statement! Mining camps in fact are suspended in an unsophisticated void between cheerful obscenity and an idealism as hopeful as Fosworthy's own. But he accepted my excuse as plausible, and calmed down.

So I was able to persist with tactful questioning and obtained some account of his doings. He assured me that he had been very cautious, avoiding Undine's home and friends and waiting for a chance to waylay her in the street. As soon as he succeeded, it was no longer necessary to visit Bath, for she was willing to meet him in Bristol or halfway. Twice she had tea with him. Once he took her to a theater. Once they had a morning together in the river meadows of the Avon.

"And did you come directly back by train to London?"

"Yes, from Bristol, where I said farewell to her. And then very carefully I called on you last night. But you weren't in."

It sounded like a child's reproach.

"And how did you spend today?"

"Quietly in my room. I telephoned to her by previous arrangement to tell her that I had arrived and to express my devotion. She replied shortly that she herself was coming to London and that I should book a room for her at my hotel. I blame myself for not reminding her at once that she would be compromised, but I was so overjoyed and she sounded so agitated that I did not. After her arrival this afternoon I wished to see you and confide in you instantly. I was very conscious, however, that I owed it to you to wait until dark."

Dark! He was hypnotized by words and conventions. As if he could not be followed in the excellent street lighting of London! He probably turned up his coat collar and pulled his hat over his eyes, making himself more conspicuous still.

It was now certain that there really had been an attempt to remove me. The coat alone did not prove beyond doubt that I had received and helped Barnabas Fosworthy; he might have chucked it into the boot of the car himself, rather than into a ditch. Similarly, my indiscretion to the bank manager could have an innocent explanation: that I had guessed, by putting two and two together, the name of the man whom Aviston-

Tresco had chased through the haunted darkness of the Mendips. But when, on the previous night, Fosworthy had been followed to my address, there was no longer any reason to hesitate.

"Is Miss Carlis connected with all these former associates of yours?" I asked.

"No! No!" he exclaimed. "If she were, I could never have risked all this. As it was, I had to be especially careful, since she has a female friend who heard, I fear, my original rejection of our beliefs and was most displeased by it, but she had no reason to guess the identity of the cause of my emotion."

"Why shouldn't your Cynthia have told her?"

"Because I asked her not to, and she willingly gave me her word."

Well, I couldn't complain. He had warned me when he was at Hammersmith that his whole object in life was to be with his enchantress. My only hope was that she felt the affinity nonsense as strongly as he did. But it seemed most unlikely.

"So this friend of hers is in touch with Aviston-Tresco?"

"You know his name?"

"Of course I do," I answered impatiently. "What I don't know is why he has it in for you. Didn't you tell me that when you were struggling through that hedge he got hold of your foot?"

"For a moment. But I was kicking."

"Did he apologize?"

"No. I am sure he only meant to put me back in confinement until he got what he wanted from me. How do you know about the Apology?"

"Poor little pussycat, for one thing," I replied obscurely.

"You should show respect for earnestly held beliefs until you know enough to confute them, Yarrow. That is your only fault," he said, getting up. "But I see you are tired."

"What hotel are you staying at?"

"The Pavilion in Bayswater. But propriety demands that I should spend the night elsewhere. I shall return to Petunia Avenue and make it, in military parlance, my headquarters. Love unconquerable in battle! Doubtless you remember your Sophocles?"

I replied rather sourly — for I felt extremely sore — that I doubted if Roman generals would approve of his tactics. He found it necessary to inform me that Sophocles was Greek, and mercifully let it go at that.

Perhaps I should have accompanied him, but by this time I felt unable to move anywhere but to bed. I warned him that he really ought to assume that he might be followed, and recommended a few quick changes of the Underground, entering or leaving trains just as the doors were closing. That should do the trick. If he was being tailed, it was, after all, by one or two complete amateurs, not by experienced detectives.

Next morning I felt much better and was able to hobble about more easily. At breakfast I was called up by a woman. She had a pleasant but rather too decided voice.

"My name is Filk," she said. "Miss Filk. Dr. Dunton advised me to call on you to discuss a very personal matter."

I replied that I was unfortunately laid up with a touch of sciatica which prevented me from inviting her to lunch, and that I should be delighted if she would come round and have a drink about midday.

There was nothing else I could do — short of saying that I refused to be interviewed except in the presence of police. It was just possible that she did come from Dunton, though I doubted it. She might be the patient he had mentioned who had given him half her confidence and was inclined to see little foxes in blots.

Whoever she was, I suspected that she was coming to negotiate on behalf of Aviston-Tresco, with a foot somehow in both camps. In that case I had a chance to convince her that I did not know and was not particularly anxious to know why my pub-keeping or supposed prospecting or any other activity was alarming them, and that the Quantocks would suit me just as well as the Mendips for my future hotel.

I then telephoned 34 Petunia Avenue and asked for Mr. Smith — pártly to satisfy myself that he was all right, partly to see what he knew of Miss Filk. The landlady told me that he had gone away over a week ago, leaving no address. But hadn't he, I asked, returned last night? No, he hadn't.

I did not like that at all. I could only hope that Undine had told him not to be a fool and that he had remained at the Pavilion Hotel after all. I called them up. Mr. Fosworthy had come in late, paid his bill and left. Was Miss Cynthia Carlis there? Yes, she was. At the mention of her, the male voice from the reception desk at once took on a tone of cordiality, even of enthusiasm. I guessed that there was still another would-be collector of blue willow pattern.

Telephoning for a taxi, I directed the driver to Notting Hill Underground station, which was not far from the Pavilion. I kept an eye on the back window and made sure that no car was following. I also waited in the station and watched out for loiterers. As soon as I was certain that no one was taking any interest in my movements, I limped to the hotel.

The porter was helpful. Mr. Fosworthy had left on foot, carrying the small bag which was his only luggage. He had, I gathered, tipped generously, asking the porter to take the greatest care of Miss Carlis and saying that he would look in after breakfast to see how she was. He had not yet arrived.

This demanded immediate action. The disappearance of Fosworthy was a plain fact, as Aviston-Tresco's attempt on me was not. The police could be called in and told the little I knew. I wish to God that I had done so then and there, but I thought it best to find out first what Cynthia Carlis had to say.

I sent up my name with a message that I was an old friend of Barnabas Fosworthy and would much like a word with her in the lounge. She came down almost at once — not in the least bothered about Fosworthy but evidently eager to gossip with someone who knew him.

To my eyes she looked a lot less fragile and more normal than at the hospital dance, for she was dressed in an expensive and countrified sweater with a rolled neck. One was only conscious of very transparent, white skin on her forehead and below her ears, and there was little temptation for the middle-aged to speculate on the extent of the network. She was also rather older than I had thought, though well under thirty.

I introduced myself and made it sound as if I had known her Barnabas from childhood. Then I told her, to see how she would react, that he had called on me the previous night and asked me if I knew of a respectable chaperone.

"Oh, isn't that like him!" she exclaimed with a laugh which I found artificial. "He's such an absurd darling! Do you know that he actually left for another hotel?"

I replied that I did not. I had no intention of mentioning his disappearance until I knew how and where she entered the story. For the moment Petunia Avenue and Mr. Smith were no business of hers. So I merely asked what time she expected him to return.

"He said he would be here at half past nine precisely," she replied. "But you know his habit of looking round corners to see what is following him. I expect that is just what he's doing and that he has lost himself."

"Did you always find him like that?" I asked.

"Losing himself? Well, he's so absentminded."

"I meant the looking round corners."

"Yes, except the first time we were out together. I thought it was just one of his peculiarities — things that make him different and rather attractive."

"Nothing else?"

She hesitated and admitted: "Well, there was a friend of mine whom neither of us much wanted to see."

Obviously innocent! She knew nothing and was not being used. So I decided to go on playing the part of old and trusted friend and find out what the devil she was up to. I did not for a moment believe that she was in love with Fosworthy. If she had been, she would have managed to convince him that his duty was to stay with her, separate rooms or not, instead of treating his mannerisms as a joke.

I ordered some drinks while we waited for the lover who was not going to arrive, and let her interrogate me about his character and background. She seemed the sort of woman who is incurious about the depth of our earthy roots, content to loiter through life in a complicated surface daze. Well, if appearance reflects character, I suppose that is about all one could expect from a water nymph. Weakness.

Yet, fluttery and irresponsible though I found her, I could not forget the kindness and self-possession with which she had treated the poor old flat-earth mathematician. The fact was that her graceful body looked so sensitive and her manners were so automatically good that they covered up her lack of intelligence. In a way she represented, like Fosworthy, a continuance of the best provincial society at the turn of the century.

I wonder how far she realized that Fosworthy's own manners concealed an insanity of love. She may have seen their relationship as sweetly sentimental — like that, say, between some college student and her much older tutor. She possibly went so far as to speculate about a gentle physical affair, but had no intention of having one.

"I like Barnabas very much and I am so sorry for him," she said.

"How did you first come across him?"

"At a meeting of the Arimathaeans in Bath."

She told me about it. Fosworthy had insisted on holding the floor. It seemed to be his habit to appear as a minority of one. He was deferred to. I doubt if I ever appreciated his importance as a local oracle. It accounted for the fury of his disciples when he denied his own teachings.

This society, however, had nothing to do with his sect; it was semi-literary with a dash of archaeology, harmlessly and romantically occupying itself with the real and mythical history of Bath and the Mendips: Arthur and Avalon, of course, the supernatural discovery of the plans of Glastonbury Abbey, and so forth.

Fosworthy had been disrespectful about the Christmas-flowering thorn supposedly sprung from the staff of Joseph of Arimathaea. He suggested that this variety had been among the first shrubs to colonize the tundra after the retreat of the ice, and still required cold to flower. He became excited and eloquent on the marvel of this thorn to Paleolithic man and emphasized the vast antiquity of folk memory.

Undine's account was naturally incoherent; but that she could repeat the subject matter at all showed that then and there she had been oddly impressed by Fosworthy. Well, of course she had. He had never taken his

adoring eyes off her. When they had their first tête-à-
tête she had been fascinated by his gentle, ceremonious
devotion. His eccentricity did not alarm her. She accepted him as the conventional, comic figure of absentminded professor.

"Your friend is also interested in primitive religion?"
I asked.

"I don't know what she is interested in," Undine replied sharply, "besides breeding dogs and killing animals or not killing them or something. Men are so absurd. Women, I mean."

The slip of the tongue passed right over my head at
the time. But it seemed a good moment to get her to talk
about herself instead of Fosworthy.

"It was sweet of you to come to London to see him," I
said. "What made you decide so suddenly?"

"Because I shall do what I like."

I apologized. I assured her that it was only my personal affection for Barnabas which had made me put so
impertinent a question.

"It wasn't impertinent at all," she answered graciously. "You have every right to ask. It was someone
else I was thinking of."

"This friend of yours?"

"How did you guess? Yes, she was following me and
she saw me say good-bye to Barnabas on Bristol station.
And then we had a row. So when Barnabas telephoned
me yesterday, I decided I would come to London."

"Have you told her where he was staying?"

"No! She doesn't know where I am either," she added
with a shade of satisfaction.

Well, if she didn't, she soon would; but that was no business of mine. I had got all I wanted, so I pleaded a previous appointment which prevented my waiting any longer for Barnabas and said an affectionate good-bye as gallantly as I could manage.

My intention now was to see this Miss Filk and insist on her accompanying me to the nearest police station. I arrived back at my flat with quarter of an hour in hand and limped up to the flat roof of the building, from which one had an extensive view of my own street and two side streets. I wanted to make certain that she was alone and that no monkey business was being planned under cover of her visit.

I spotted the probable Miss Filk when she was fifty yards away on the opposite pavement. She was dressed in a black town suit, smart but severe, with a man's cravat round her throat, and wearing a simple felt hat. Pacing alongside her on a slack lead was a magnificent black Doberman — a very effective chaperone when committing oneself to the flat of a stranger. It occurred to me that I should have to be pretty tactful if I meant to detain her against her will.

As soon as I saw her examine the street numbers and wait to cross the road, I hopped fast down the stairs with the aid of the banisters and was inside my front door before she rang. She was in her late thirties, taller than I had thought and authoritative. She struck me as a woman of experience with whom it might be possible to talk frankly without bringing police — or Dobermans — too crudely into the picture.

I supplied her with sherry and cigarettes — she

puffed continuously and aggressively — and admired the dog. She said that she bred them. I then expressed my admiration of Dr. Dunton, though by now I was sure that she had only used his name as a passport. Her response was curt, so I left a pause for her to open up.

"A Mr. Fosworthy," she said, "has been making himself a nuisance to my ward."

So that was it. The wardship was rather out of my depth. I could, however, understand it when I remembered the devastating effect which Cynthia Carlis had on some of my sex. It was more than likely that in early youth one or two of her contemporaries had been far too brutal. And then there were the rest of us who stared at her with an almost insulting absence of desire. She must have found men cruel and unaccountable. Even more convincing than anything else was the fact that Fosworthy, being Fosworthy, would of course have set his guileless heart on a girl who was unattainable.

He had had, from his point of view, a damnable stroke of bad luck, caught out by his innocence, not by any carelessness. His Undine ought to have foreseen that Miss Filk was likely to become suspicious about her mysterious absences. Perhaps she did foresee it, didn't care, even welcomed it. After all, she could not know that the looking round corners was deadly serious.

And so Miss Filk, after jealously trailing Undine to Bristol station and skulking behind a barrowload of fish boxes or racing pigeons or whatever was handy, had been doubly shocked to find that her secret rival was a man and that the man was the missing Fosworthy. I take it that her first action was to warn Aviston-Tresco or some other associate that she had sighted him on the London train, and that later in the day she had such a flaming row with her "ward" that the girl walked out on her.

Even so, Fosworthy's trail could never have been recovered if they had not been so obsessed by his connection with me. The gaps were now easy to fill in. Somebody had obtained my address, cautiously watched my flat and spotted Fosworthy's first visit. That gave time for Aviston-Tresco to arrange the front seat of his van and to organize whatever simple trick would be enough to fool Fosworthy. It was a hundred to one that after his second visit to my flat he had again been put out of circulation.

"Miss Filk, I'm not going to pretend to you," I said. "I am sure you are well aware of the circumstances in which I met Mr. Fosworthy."

"He is quite mad, you know."

"He is certainly eccentric when he talks about your ward. Otherwise I find him reliable for so quixotic a person."

"You believe what he has told you?"

"He hasn't told me anything except that he suddenly found his feeling for Miss Carlis getting in the way of some personal creed of his."

It was only then that I noticed an unsteady brilliance in her eyes. I warned myself that I had better be careful. Whether she had come to negotiate or not, she was in a savage temper and more likely to blow up than to listen.

"Then why have you financed him?"

"I have not exactly financed him. I lent him money because he was obviously in trouble and I couldn't help liking him. I am very sorry that he can't keep away from your ward, but it was not my primary intention to make things easier for him."

"I am quite sure it was not."

She said this slowly and contemptuously, and I thought it was time to give her something which could be passed back.

"I'm a working mining engineer, Miss Filk," I assured her, "and I know the geology of the Mendips and what one can or can't expect to find there without being told by Mr. Fosworthy. Really you can leave him out of it."

As I see now, I could not have said anything worse. It looked as if I had learned all that Fosworthy could betray, and was making a futile attempt to protect him by admitting it.

There was an awkward pause, so I leaned forward to scratch the ears of the supercilious dog. I have a faint recollection of raising my head in alarm. Probably the blow was already on its way downwards.

The next thing I knew was that I lay on the floor of a van with a pillow under my head. To my newly opened eyes it seemed to be quite dark. This worried me until, through the back window, I saw lights flashing past. I stayed quiet, except for slightly shaking my head to see that it belonged to me.

It was a fair guess that I had been coshed by Miss Filk. Never having been coshed before, I could not tell how efficiently she had done it. I felt more drowsy than ill, so that I knew she could not have hit me hard enough to lay me out for more than a few minutes. Without actually knowing what happened, I assume that Miss Filk had come provided with a syringe to keep me quiet. As a breeder of sleek, expensive Dobermans she was probably quite accustomed to using it.

How they carried me out of my flat after Miss Filk had telephoned that she had got me I do not know, but again it is not difficult to guess. I lived only one floor up, and most of the other tenants were out all day at their places of business. No one was likely to see my removal from flat to front door. For the short passage from front door to van — well, it wouldn't be beyond Aviston-Tresco's powers to provide an official-looking stretcher and a couple of St. John's Ambulance caps.

My wrists and ankles were firmly tied. I was not gagged, but it was pointless to start yelling and be forcibly suppressed when I could not be clearly heard from any passing car. On the other side of the van was a bundle, snoring. I could just make out the untidy mass of fair hair at one end. I regarded the drugged Fosworthy with mixed feelings. I was sorry for him. I was glad of his companionship. But I was certain that if he could make matters worse, he would.

I must have dozed off again, for the next thing I remember is Fosworthy sitting up and looking at me. He had something soft stuffed into his mouth and held in place by a scarf tied behind his neck. He made a complicated, indignant gesture with his head, which I took as meaning that this was an outrage and that he would declare my absolute innocence. Soon afterwards the van bumped along a field track or unmetaled lane. Fosworthy evidently recognized the uneven motion, for he nodded to me as much as to say that he knew where we were. I can't see what comfort he got from it.

We stopped, all lights off, on a concrete yard outside a farm building. Aviston-Tresco and Jedder got down from the front seats and opened up the van. I could dimly make out some water troughs and a clamp of silage. I had the impression of a lonely barn in some outlying part of the estate.

"I do not want to cause you unnecessary pain," Aviston-Tresco said to me, "but if you shout I shall gag you at once."

I said nothing. Anyway I doubted if there were a living soul within earshot. The southwest wind carried the softness of the Bristol Channel, and I could sense that it was sweeping over bare downland without trees or buildings, for it was steady as at sea and silent except for the whispering through grass. Everything suggested that we were on the Mendips, almost certainly on some desolate hill pasture of Jedder's farm.

The pair of them carried me in, dropped me gently on a hard floor and went back for Fosworthy. As soon as he, too, was safely inside the building, Jedder locked the door and switched on a light.

The place appeared to have been fairly recently converted from an old stone barn. There were glass lights in the roof, but no windows. The double door through which we had come was new and fitted closely. There was a second door — an ordinary house door — opposite. Along one of the side walls were piled bales of hay.

The other was occupied by old, disintegrating cow stalls. On a floor of rolled rubble were some agricultural implements, an aluminum ladder, a disused tractor, a discarded dynamo and bits and pieces from former days when horses had been used on the farm.

Yet the barn was plainly for more than shelter and storage, since there were two twelve-volt batteries to provide light, and an iron stove with a stack of wood alongside it. As I learned afterwards, Jedder's farm-hands were aware that he and his friends visited the place for picnics or meetings; but eccentricities were none of their business so long as their wages were paid.

When Fosworthy's gag was out, he let loose his indignation as if Aviston-Tresco and Jedder were a couple of impudent trespassers. He showed not a sign of fear, though whether that was due to his beliefs or his anger at being humiliated I could not tell.

"I protest against your treatment of my generous and kindly friend, which is intolerable," he declared. "The position in which he finds himself is entirely my fault."

"It is," said Aviston-Tresco.

"But I have told him nothing! I merely explained to him, as I have to you, that I consider a number of our basic tenets need restating."

He might have been a sacked commissar defending himself before his interrogators — except that I doubt if any political fanatic could be so romantically self-sufficient.

"You threatened us," Jedder reminded him.

"Certainly I threatened you! I said that if you refused to listen to me I should make the whole thing public."

They were of the same height and roughly of the same coloring, though Jedder must have weighed half as much again. The two crests of fair hair jerked at each other.

"And then you went straight to Yarrow."

"I had never seen him before in my life."

"Frankly, Barnabas, I don't know," Aviston-Tresco said. "But when you did talk to him he realized that what you were proclaiming in your usual excitable way could be worth a lot of money to a man looking for a hotel site."

That absolutely beat me, for I had been certain that they distrusted me as a former mining engineer. It was beyond imagination that Fosworthy could know anything of interest to the catering industry except a recipe for dandelion leaf sauce.

"I give you my word that I have told him no more than I had to in order that he should understand my intellectual predicament," Fosworthy replied in a tone which suggested that his word could not possibly be disbelieved.

I must have smiled. He was an incredible man. What he said was quite true, but his intellectual predicament was the last thing I took seriously.

"Then why did he lend you money?"

"Because I had to escape. I have now a great deal to live for."

"I had no intention of violence, only of confining you again until you came to your senses and we could decide what to do with you. But just look what your emotional idiocy has landed us in now!" Aviston-Tresco exclaimed. "Yarrow must dissolve and you, my poor, dear Barnabas, as well."

He sounded exasperated. Nothing more than exasperated. That revealed to me more clearly than any of Dunton's or Fosworthy's attempts at explanation how sincerely these people believed that death was an unimportant incident. Aviston-Tresco's manner did not belong to anything so serious as murder. It was that, say, of a creditor telling us that we were such incompetent fools that there was nothing left for him to do but to take legal proceedings.

"What earthly chance do you think you have of getting away with it?" I asked from the floor. "You must have left enough clues for the stupidest of policemen."

"They will not find any motive for your dissolution, Mr. Yarrow, or any body either. The only clue is a car with false number plates from which you were transferred to my van."

I kept my mouth shut about the doctor who stitched me up, because it seemed unfair to set these lunatics on him. For the same reason I did not mention Dunton. In any case neither of them would be surprised or suspicious if they never saw me again. But if I had realized that I was within seconds of what they chose to call dissolution, I should have shouted at him that he was not as safe as he thought.

"Again I tell you that I am very sorry," he said with a smile that was an obscenity in its gentleness and confidence.

"Again?" Jedder asked.

"He is doomed already. But we won't wait for it."

"When? Why?"

Aviston-Tresco was embarrassed and evidently did not know what to reply. It was an eye-opener that he had never told Jedder — and that went for Miss Filk too — of his first attempt on me.

The order of events became a little clearer. What he had hoped was that after the prick I would accompany him to his club for a drink and go home unsuspecting. The fact that I knew all about his Apology badly shook him. He panicked. He had never tried to watch my movements when I bolted for that public lavatory and had cleared out as fast as he could. It was not surprising. Hundreds of animals he had kindly and graciously put out of pain, but this was the first human being.

Then he had to improvise a plan for silencing me before I was removed to hospital. I might also go to the police. No doubt Miss Filk had been warned to take no action if I showed the slightest sign of having set a trap. But, by and large, he was confident that I was a man of independent character who would be most unwilling to make accusations without a scrap of sensible evidence.

It did not look as if he had even examined my backside in the hurry of kidnapping me. If he had, he must have spotted that I had never cleaned and sewed up the wound myself. He took the sciatica which Miss Filk must have reported as the beginning of the end.

While I lay tied up, wondering whether my dissolution would be by syringe, knife or what, all this raced through my head, all logically following from the fact that Aviston-Tresco had deceived his associates. I would never claim to have thought it out. My analysis was more like a continuity of street scenes passing before the eyes.

Alan Jedder did not like Aviston-Tresco's admission at all, for he realized that there might be other evidence lying about to be picked up besides false number plates.

"You'd better tell me the whole story," he said. "They will be all right here."

The pair went through the door into the next room or compartment, and I could faintly hear their voices. Jedder's confidence that I would be "all right" was justified. I am always inclined to accept a situation which I cannot alter, and the aftermath of the sedative made me more so than usual.

But one could not bind Fosworthy's flame with ropes. So long as this world held Undine, he was not prepared to be dissolved into another. He rolled over onto his side and started to propel himself across the floor like the nonexistent broken-backed pussy. He wriggled his shoulders up against an old plowshare which was leaning by the wall and began to saw his wrists back and forth. I was terrified lest he should knock it over; but for once he had single-minded control of his clumsiness. Then he untied his feet and released me.

We were locked in and Jedder had pocketed the key of the outer door, so there was nothing for it but violence. I grabbed Aviston-Tresco's powerful electric torch, which he had obligingly left on the bonnet of the tractor together with his hat and a sinister instrument bag, and picked up a pitchfork with a broken handle. It was a frightening weapon, for the two prongs had rusted away to fine points. A man would have to have his antitetanus injections up-to-date after a poke in the belly with those.

"I apprehend that you mean to take life," Fosworthy whispered.

"I shall duly apologize," I said.

But I was far from happy about it. The law allows one to use reasonable force. How much was reasonable for a person who could establish that he was kidnapped, but might have difficulty in proving that his life had ever been in danger?

Fosworthy told me that there was another way out of the building, earnestly explaining that he considered his first duty must be to protect me. I replied patiently that I wholly agreed and that we should run for the nearest police station as fast as we could.

"I greatly fear there will be no chance of that as yet," he said. "Can you hold the door for a minute or two?"

I doubted it. My own unaided efforts, while still dopey from Miss Filk's cosh and a sedative, were not enough to hold the door against two healthy men. Any attempt to drag something heavy across the floor would be heard. However, there was always the pitchfork.

Fosworthy started to lift bales of hay from the center of the stack against the wall. With his height and long arms, he had just the build for the job, and he worked like a demon. In less than a minute he had made a considerable bay, and was down to the two bottom layers. The bales were a helpful protection for the door. I was silently building them into a wall when the main stack collapsed inward with thuds which were loud enough to hear.

Aviston-Tresco and Jedder at once charged the door. My wall of hay was little use. There was nothing solid I could get my feet against, and no doubt I instinctively spared the muscles of my left thigh. Meanwhile Fosworthy had cleared away the fallen bales and was heaving at the bottom row.

The door gradually opened. Aviston-Tresco got his right arm and shoulder through, and there was nothing for it but the pitchfork. I was savage enough to hope that it had last been used for shifting manure. It went in at his wrist, the tine reaching as far as the elbow. I tried to withdraw it and twisted the curved tine in the process. His scream appalled me. I wouldn't have thought that such a noise could come from a man's throat.

I slammed the door shut. Fosworthy shouted to me to come over quick. He had cleared the floor and opened a thick wooden hatch set in rough brickwork. I saw him hang onto the rim of the shaft and drop. The hole was immediately flooded with light. I dashed across to it and let go into space. Fosworthy tried to break my fall, with the result that we were both shaken and bruised. Jedder, yards behind me, did not attempt to follow. He slammed the hatch shut.

The passage into which we had crashed was a gallery driven through earth and loose limestone, shored in a very amateurish way. To my professional eye the roof looked most unsafe. The gallery extended for over thirty feet, lit by two naked bulbs, and ended at a steep, nearly vertical slope which was clearly not artificial though the stone had been hacked about to remove projections. Down this led a flight of stairs — obviously a brow or companion ladder from a ship — with stout brass-mounted steps and a teak handrail.

We were now in a small, irregular cavern. It was partly furnished with a table and a few chairs. Along the wall was a rack on which were hanging some sheepskin coats, fleece-lined. There were even a mirror and a washbasin, showing that this was a sort of cloakroom or changing room. In a horizontal cleft was a range of storage batteries for the light. Since they must have been charged from the surface, it was plain that the dynamo and tractor in the barn were not so unserviceable as they had been made to appear.

"I must hope that the cry was due to surprise rather than extreme pain," Fosworthy said, breaking the silence. "I trust this is all worth the trouble. If only you could see her!"

One could hardly imagine a remark less appropriate to the situation. But I had to take him as he was. I answered that I had seen her, that there couldn't be two.

"Where?" he asked eagerly. "What did you think?"

I shrank instinctively from telling him of my visit to the Pavilion and of Miss Filk. He would be overcome by fear for his Cynthia and remorse that his innocent ecstasy on Bristol station had betrayed me. She and I must have been the only close friends left who returned his affection — one of us with complete, if exasperated sincerity; the other with, at any rate, pity. So I merely mentioned Dr. Dunton and the dance.

He said that Dunton was an excellent fellow, though limited, very limited — which certainly meant that the doctor had at some time tried to preach common sense to him.

"And now, would you mind telling me where we are?"

"We are in the largest cavern of the Mendips," he said. "This is the secret."

"But why?"

He did not answer. They seemed to be as unaccountable as twelve-year-olds. All right, a private cave! So what? It was under Jedder's land, and nobody could compel him to repeat the vulgarities of Cheddar if he didn't want to.

"And how do we get out?"

"I fear I had to take too sudden a decision," Fosworthy replied. "That question did occur to me, only to be dismissed as momentarily irrelevant."

"You mean, we can't get out except by the way we came in?"

"I would not put it as strongly as that, but it might turn out to be so."

"Then I think we had better fight our way out now, while only Jedder is up top."

"He will, I am sure, have replaced the bales of hay. And in any case we cannot reach the hatch without a ladder."

So that was what the aluminum ladder in the barn was for!

"But in that case we are trapped."

"We may indeed have to endure hunger," Fosworthy remarked mildly. "To be alone here is unnerving. But surely much can be done when there are two of us to-gether?"

The situation was plain disaster. If I had not been well used to the silence and drip of mines, I should have panicked. Even so I sounded shrill to myself as I put a vital question to Fosworthy. No, he answered, the lights could not be turned off from the surface. The switch for the gallery lights was at the bottom of the shaft, and the rest were controlled from the changing room.

"If I have understood the dialogue correctly," he said, "Tom Aviston-Tresco believes you will dissolve down here long before starvation does the same for me. In that case, thinking that I must be alone and harmless, he may take steps to find me and put me out of pain. Perhaps you would tell me why he is so sure you are doomed?"

I told him. He tut-tutted.

"And I was convinced that I had protected you com-pletely!" he exclaimed. "Bless me, you must be in some discomfort! And I kept you standing so long last night!"

I did indeed feel sore the moment he mentioned it. I took down the mirror from the wall to inspect the dam-age. There was surprisingly little. That young doctor had done a good job. His plaster was still in place, though blood was oozing over the top of it where a stitch may have pulled out. My head was still very ten-der from Miss Filk's fortunately ladylike blow, but I felt in fair condition. If anything remained of the drug, fear and violent action had blown it out of my system.

"How did you get picked up?" I asked.

"I really cannot understand it at all. I did just what you told me, only I took a bus to the Pavilion instead of the Underground. I walked away from the hotel intending to take another bus to Hammersmith and was waiting at the stop when a woman drove up and asked if I would like a lift. I thought it most kind of her, and a great stroke of luck that she chanced to be going my way. It was getting late and I knew that the landlady at 34 Petunia Avenue is accustomed to retire at eleven."

I interrupted impatiently to ask what had happened. Didn't he recognize the driver?

"No, she was quite unknown to me. Of course I am not very familiar with London, but after a while I began to feel that we were not on the right road for Hammersmith. She stopped on a common somewhere, which I observed with growing anxiety was entirely deserted. Then I was seized, with a hand over my mouth, and I knew no more, as they say. I should never have suspected Tom Aviston-Tresco of having such powers of organization."

He didn't need any. When Fosworthy turned up at my flat for the second time, all he had to do was to whistle up one of Miss Filk's little friends with a car and a winning manner. Even so, something had gone wrong. Fosworthy had managed to reach his hotel, and while they were waiting outside thinking that the operation was off for the night and perhaps for good, damned if his preposterous chivalry didn't make him walk out again!

As for the car driver, no doubt Miss Filk had dreamed up some romantic story to keep her mouth shut. Anything plausible would do, for she was not going to hear any more of her passenger. Police would not waste time in serious investigation just because so erratic a person had disappeared, nor newspapers be tempted to publish a photograph of him.

Silence and cold. Drip and echo. A loneliness where there was not even so distant a cousin as a scrap of plant life for company. I took down one of the sheepskin coats and put it on.

"Who made all this?" I asked.

"Alan Jedder and one or two others. I helped."

Fosworthy showed me Jedder's tool store. It was well equipped with crowbars, picks and shovels, and plenty of electrical spare parts. I also found two coils of instantaneous fuse and a box of detonators. Unfortunately there were no explosives.

We took a pick and a crowbar with us. Fosworthy led the way along a lighted passage, twisting, sometimes very narrow, sometimes opening out into considerable caves, and never going downhill for long. Aviston-Tresco's torch, flashed into the clefts and dark holes along our path, showed that many of them dropped away into the heart of the hills. At one point the track was tilted towards a terrifying abyss, but wide enough for reasonable safety.

The place was a typical limestone cave of unknown dimensions. In fact most of them are of unknown dimensions until the potholers get busy; even then picks and ropes or an underwater dive will nearly always reveal more. We had traveled something over six hundred yards when we came to the last of the lights. It was above the entrance to a low, wide cleft on the right of the path. I threw a beam into it, but could distinguish nothing. We then climbed a steep slope where there was dry earth underfoot instead of rock glazed by a film of stalagmite.

"This is the other way out, but we blocked it," Fosworthy said. "I am very concerned lest we may have done it too thoroughly."

So was I. A big boulder looked as if it could be persuaded to roll downhill until I saw that it was held in position by smooth faces of concrete on which my pick rang and jarred.

"How far to the surface?" I asked.

"Seventeen and a half feet," Fosworthy replied precisely.

"What does the entrance look like from outside?"

"It cannot be seen. We spread earth over rubble and planted grass and an elder in it."

"Is there any other way out?"

"Jedder has never discovered one. But let us hope there is."

Hope! The only hope was up the shaft and through the hatch, bales or no bales, and I wish I had recognized it then and there.

It would have taken a week to move the boulder with such tools as we had, and we should only come to more concrete, Fosworthy said. The sides of the passage, weatherworn before the entrance was blocked, were more promising. Fosworthy took over from me and valiantly wielded a pick. Every blow was driven home with the force of his obsession. Love unconquerable in battle!

We went on for hours, but it became plainer and plainer that all we were doing was to dig a tunnel under a roof of solid limestone. Eventually we came up against a wall of sound rock at our working face. We should have died of starvation before we ever got through.

We resumed our sheepskin coats and drank from a dark, icy pool where drips had collected. Then we walked wearily back along the lighted passage to try the hatch. In the changing room and the shored gallery the silence sang, neutral as the grave and as indifferent to our presence. We could not reach the hatch in spite of a crazy erection of balks of timber and the table. Fosworthy, taller than I, just touched it before our scaffolding collapsed. Even if it hadn't, a hand — with no firm foothold beneath — was useless against half a ton of hay.

During a long rest to recover some strength, we considered the only two courses open to us. We could wait in the changing room indefinitely until Jedder and his friends opened the hatch, or we could explore the whole cave system at the risk of losing ourselves. Putting my trust in surprise, I wanted to switch off the lights and wait, though I doubted my own patience to endure such blind emptiness.

Fosworthy voted for exploration. He would. He was always an optimist when plunging at the unknown. Still, he had a case. He thought it might be days before anyone opened the hatch. That was not altogether consistent with his belief that Aviston-Tresco would come and put him out of pain as soon as the arm had been treated, but I gave way to him. Anything was better than sitting still.

All he knew was that Jedder had come across a stream. Well, that was encouraging. But it did not have to emerge on the surface; it could seep into marsh or spring up into the bed of one of the many lowland brooks. The complex of Cheddar caves was too far away for any connection to be discoverable. The extent of Wookey Hole and the other smaller caverns of the Mendips was known. I was inclined to think that the exit, if any, would be beneath the northeastern escarpment, since any considerable spring bursting out of the limestone on the southwest would have been thoroughly investigated by local landowners hoping for another tourist gold mine.

In the tool store Fosworthy found three lanterns, clean and full up with paraffin. A second useful discovery was a compass, which at least would allow me the illusion that I was going somewhere. We had no string, and the only rope, wound on the drum of a winch, was not long enough to be worth taking. The next best thing, though far too heavy, was a drum of electric flex. We carried this between us on a crowbar through the middle and set off.

I found that the lighted passage ran very roughly west. Only one of the openings on the northern side offered a practicable route, leading us down until we came to a great bubble in the rock not far from the blocked entrance, but on a lower level. There were several clefts in the walls. One of them, which we could just pass on hands and knees, gave access to a more open system with magnificent stalactites like the ranged pipes of a cathedral organ. This was the time to start paying out flex. I had trouble already in identifying the hole by which we had entered.

We chose the easiest passage, again running sharply downhill, and soon found that without ropes our movements were very limited. Fosworthy was eager to climb down tunnels which were far too dangerous. Once committed to the choice of a northward direction, he was like a child in convincing himself that it must be right. But I wasn't permitting any such rashness. I had experience of shafts which could be descended by jumps, drops and slithers and were utterly impossible to climb.

So we had to go where we could and accept the frequent compass readings which insisted that we had traveled round in a circle or a figure of eight. When the flex ran out we were heading southwest and had probably crossed the line of the lighted passage at least one hundred feet beneath it.

The wash of a stream was now faintly audible, though hard to distinguish from the hissing of ears in the sepulchral silence. A distant plop of water from the roof could be startling as a live presence, and I would search for it with the beam of the torch. Outside the tiny circle of our lanterns, there was no such thing as direction. Not even sound had direction.

We left one of the lanterns standing on the now empty drum of flex and made our way cautiously to the edge of the water. It was running smoothly in a channel some six feet below the older terrace on which we stood and did not seem of sufficient volume to force a way out at the foot of the hills. It did flow northeast, however.

As far as my beam reached, the terrace offered no difficulty, continuing along the right bank under a roof of widely varying height. I went back to fetch the lantern and put it down to mark the small orifice through which we had come to the water. Between that point and the end of the flex there was no possibility of losing the way.

We set out along the course of the stream and may have traveled a quarter of a mile before it vanished down a hole in the floor of an irregular cavern of immense height. Leaving this sluice behind and on our left, we came to a tunnel leading steeply upwards. Water had been running down it, and I was convinced by the deposit of mud that it was surface water, possibly overflowing from spring or marsh in winter. It was blazing lunacy to follow this tempting pothole without flex to find the way back. But every despairing move we made was lunacy.

I still think that we were on a route to the surface which could have been managed by a properly equipped expedition. Fosworthy and I, however, were stopped by a sudden and slippery rise in the pothole. We dreamed of it as a sure ladder to the blessed sky, but were helpless. The next thirty feet of rock were sheer.

We turned back. I had been carefully registering the few openings out of our tunnel and had no fear of losing the way; in any case we had the deposit left by the winter torrent as a guide. Eventually we reached the flats where the stream disappeared and followed the terrace on the right bank expecting to pick up the light of the lantern at any minute. We did not pick it up. Instead, we came to a rock fall which we had certainly never crossed.

Obviously there were two streams, one a tributary of the other. We must have emerged from our pothole by a slightly different route, identified the sluice by ear rather than eye, and chosen the wrong terrace. The circle of dim light, within which were our bodies and our forlorn determination to live, had a radius which was ample in a narrow passage but inadequate in larger caverns where an area of blackness might be an opening or simply space. However sure we were that we had made no mistake, any mistake was possible.

We retraced our steps to try to find the correct terrace. Landmarks, such as they were, appeared unfamiliar, but that was to be expected. When approached from the opposite direction, every rock formation had a different set of shadows. At last we heard the unmistakable gurgle of the fall and arrived at it by squeezing through a slot like a couple of twisted pennies. The water was surging down from above. We were on the left bank of the stream, not the right.

My guess as to what had happened is no more good now than it was then. I had been concentrating my attention on the walls of the cave and the accidents underfoot, never turning a beam on the flow of the water. Somewhere we had reached a third tributary and followed it down.

No explanation. Nothing. It was far worse than to be lost among the involutions of some vast rock chamber when one could at least keep one's head and systematically explore the openings till they were identified. But in that sump of waters we had nothingness. Instinct, intelligence, the senses — they were all put out of action.

The worst of it was that I had been navigating by water, not by compass. I sat down and cursed — frenzied, filthy swearing. Fosworthy's reaction was astonishing.

"My dear man, the fear of dissolution is so absurd," he said. "It is nothing but a moment's suffering."

His tone was in no way unctuous, but simple, sure and comforting. However, I was in no mood for it. I remarked that when it was a question of his Cynthia, he didn't seem to enjoy more than anyone else the thought of being bloody well dissolved.

"That is different," he replied. "I am exercised by the conditions of survival, not the fact."

We rested, shivered and drank. We tried again. I cannot clearly remember much of it. My watch said that we spent five hours stumbling about aimlessly and getting physically weaker. It could have been seventeen hours, but the paraffin in the lantern would not have lasted that long. It went out, of course, at last, and we had nothing left but Aviston-Tresco's excellent electric torch.

Again we heard the fall and worked towards it. We had long since given up following the courses of streams. The fall was something we knew, somewhere to die. One's strong instinct — if I make myself plain — is not to die nowhere. The mere rediscovery comforted us a little. Fosworthy said:

"Suppose this is the bottom of the sluice which we first saw from the top."

I replied that it didn't matter if it was; we could not climb it.

"Let us assume it is," he insisted. "We are traveling in a three-dimensional world which soon we will be unable to see. We must always go uphill and, when we can, always in the direction of the fall, watching the compass as long as we have light."

It was better than giving up. The problem, of course, was how far to continue away from the fall in the hope of finding a way back towards it. The amazing thing is that we never disputed over this. I must have caught some of his gentleness.

At last we heard the gurgle of water again and knew that this time we must be well above the level of the bottom of the fall. But there was no going on. The flashlight showed a clear drop below us. At the limit of the beam was the sluice. We were looking out from a window high up in the cave which contained the original stream, unmistakably plunging downwards, the terrace we had followed, the entries to the steep pothole and presumably a bend of the tributary which had misled me.

Fosworthy was determined to attempt the descent. Myself, I would have gone on wandering rather than tackle that drop; but to him it was a shortcut with Undine somewhere at the ultimate end of it. He hurled his coat over the edge and climbed down the first twenty feet. Then he had to let go, and fall or glissade until he fetched up against a lumpy, mushroomy growth of stalagmite. He hit it and called up that he was all in one piece.

"I may by misadventure have broken a toe," he said, "but I shall be able to catch you."

I threw the torch down to him, muffled in my coat. As soon as he found it and lit up the darkness, I followed. He did not exactly break my fall. He saved my life by catching a foot as I missed the stalagmites and was shooting past him.

The rest of the descent was not difficult. We then set out along the once familiar terrace, hurrying and tripping since the torch was now dying. The lantern we had left behind was, of course, out, and we searched for it desperately until one of us fell over it. We were in bad shape, Fosworthy limping and I streaming blood from a jagged wound in the neck — the result of my head swinging round in a half-circle after Fosworthy grabbed me. The loose skin of the throat must have caught on a pointed stalagmite. The check possibly prevented a fracture of the skull, for, as it was, my jaw had thumped against rock hard enough to knock out a tooth.

We went through the same incompetent search for the end of the flex, which we were too dizzy with hunger and fatigue to find. At last we had it. In half an hour we were back in the lighted passage. We were still alive. We shivered a little less in fresh, dry coats. That was all. There was no sign that anyone had opened the hatch.

Turning off the light to save the batteries, we tried to sleep. I suppose we did, for I remember feeling suddenly stiff, sore and immovable. When I groaned Fosworthy groped his way to the light switch, audibly limping. I think he had long been lying quite still and awake. My watch read half past seven, but I was no longer certain whether we had been underground for thirty hours or forty-two.

"I have been considering your future after you have dissolved," he said placidly. "Come with me! It will help you."

The pools of dim, white light in the passage were as depressing as darkness. That crude illumination of silent rock emphasized the pitiless inhumanity of the place. As Fosworthy led me on towards the blocked entrance I reminded myself severely that we had not been long enough without food to be exhausted, and that if I had been in the outer world I should have recognized my physical distress as due to nothing but frantic activity. Consequently I began to feel that dissolution was a lot less imminent.

We came to the horizontal cleft on the right of the path, outside which was the last of the lights. Fosworthy stooped, entered and felt for a switch. Two soft floodlights at ground level and one powerful reflector overhead lit up the wearisome, eternal limestone. I could not imagine why so much trouble had been taken in a cave which was not at all remarkable except for an overhang of smooth rock like the initial curve of a dome and another irregular slope at an angle of about sixty degrees to the floor.

Then I made out the mammoth, vividly drawn in a rust-red pigment, and I swear that my first impression was not of the physical form of the animal, but of its bearing, its mood. In spite of the spears stuck in flanks and belly, it was unaggressive. It was melancholy in the moment of death, almost trusting. It received. One could well imagine that it forgave.

At first I paid no attention to the animated black lines around it and turned to the floodlit overhang covered with beasts, sometimes in groups deliberately composed, sometimes overlying each other where bosses of rock had tempted the artist into bas-relief. There were deer, bison and horses and some strange sitting creature with short, beseeching forepaws which could have been, if the painter preserved his scale, a very large squirrel or some kind of sloth. The short ears proved that it was not rabbit or hare.

The paintings were covered by the thin glaze of the limestone walls which had preserved them like the glass over a picture. A better geologist than I, who knew how long it took to form a millimeter of the deposit, could probably date the paintings within a thousand years. They belonged to the same tradition as the art of Altamira, Lascaux and the Pyrenean caves, yet they were livelier and perhaps less delicate. Movement and expression were what the artist was after, just as in the prehistoric picture galleries of the Spanish caves. But, unlike his southern contemporaries, this animal lover

— was he hunter, priest or gourmet? — did not leave out human beings, though he drew them conventionally, with no attempt at the tender realism of the animals. A lively little black figure with angular lines for arms and legs was good enough for a man.

"Now you understand," Fosworthy said. "They believed that in my distress I had told you, and that you had lent me money so that I could go into hiding and keep quiet."

I did understand. Buy your hotel, buy up any land available for the hot-dog stands, the motor coach parks and the souvenir shops, and when all is safely in the bag, send a postcard to the British Museum! No wonder Aviston-Tresco was confident that I would give nothing away to the police until I had completed my plans! The cave system — that and that alone — had puzzled me as a motive for so much desperation, since it was on Jedder's land and he could control access as he liked. But this was a possession for the whole world. It would and ought to become a place of pilgrimage.

All the same, I could only stare at Fosworthy's agitation. People were certainly going to make a lot of undeserved money when the secret was out. But what about it?

"It is not the paintings themselves," he said. "It is their profound religious significance."

This was what Dunton had got hold of. He knew the beliefs from one or more patients; he knew, as many other local inhabitants must have, of meetings; he knew of the Apology for giving death, of the fellowship with animals and the seemingly inconsistent obsession with hunting. But he had not the faintest suspicion that the small sect preserved an objective secret.

"So this is what started you off?"

"No, no!" Fosworthy exclaimed as if I had doubted his power to think independently. "Our group had been in existence for some years. Many of us were impressed by the Quakers, who are influential in this part of the county. Excellent people, but too easily content!"

He meant, I suppose, the same criticism as when he described Dunton as limited. Nobody could be more sane and healthy than Quakers; but I can well see that the mystics and eccentrics still inseparable from the Isle of Glass might find the admirable influence of the Friends too simple for them.

I gathered that Fosworthy, the bank manager and a handful of others had formed a mild vegetarian circle which used to contemplate the Unity of Life. That was the start. I wish I had listened more patiently; but when his eyes began to shine and his gestures to be too emphatic, I could only see the abnormality.

"Who found the cave?" I asked.

"Miss Filk. Her wretched Dobermans put up a fox which went to ground under a rock. Jedder, who is a keen rider to hounds, visited the place a week later to stop the earth, as I believe it is called, and made his way inside. He kept quiet about it. He saw it as a mere curiosity which he would not allow to disturb his life. Another man would have thought only of the admission fees. But Alan Jedder looks inward."

I was about to say that he wouldn't much like what he saw. But he probably did. No doubt he congratulated himself, like the rest of us, on being an individual of wonderful potentialities.

"Then one day, exploring alone, he found the paintings. He invited Aviston-Tresco and myself to see them. We all realized very soon that there was the synthesis we sought."

The earnestness of the synthesis went on and on and I tried to take it in — since Aviston-Tresco's opinions were responsible for my almost certain death — while mind and eyes were daydreaming among the lovely simplicities of human life twenty-five thousand years ago. I could see how the dying mammoth might stir the imagination of our crowded world in which an animal is a pet or a potential carcass. The recognition between hunter and hunted of the divinity in each is lost to us.

Then the lights went out. I could not think for fear. After a few seconds they came on again. I thanked God, and tried to reconstruct causes, all unlikely, of a breakdown in so elementary a system. They went out again, and stayed out.

"I told you he would look for me," Fosworthy said.

I hoped he was right and that someone had come down through the hatch and switched off the lights to immobilize us, if either of us were alive. Assuming that a fuse had gone, we had no hope of ever finding our way back along the passage. In theory it could be done by feeling for the wires, but I doubted if that would be possible in practice; there were too many openings and obstacles where the line was overhead and out of reach. In darkness the passage was merely a random route, undiscoverable except by chance. Turn round twice and that was the end.

"Where will he look?" I asked.

"If I am not near the entrance, he will look here, where of course I should choose to wait."

"And what then?"

"I presume he will help me to dissolve peacefully. He seemed certain that I should be alone."

I had forgotten the puncture from the van seat. Naturally! By now I was equally sore all over. However, I felt quite capable of waiting for a far sorer Aviston-Tresco along the track. What good it would do was more doubtful. According to Fosworthy, nobody committed himself to that labyrinth unless a companion was left at the top of the hatch.

Pulling Fosworthy by the hand, I felt my way out of the painted cave. It was the only time when he seemed reluctant to live. Perhaps the haunting influence of that calm mammoth overcame his desire for Undine. We followed the wires some little way and then turned into a confused tumble of ledges and pinnacles just off the track. I had passed it three times and knew it would give cover from any searching beam and from the passage lights. As for getting out again, one had simply to scramble downhill in any direction and follow the cave wall.

First of all we heard Aviston-Tresco's voice.

"Barnabas! My poor Barnabas! Where are you?"

It boomed and trilled and echoed and died away, once returning seconds later with a faint, uncanny "Barnabas!"

They passed the recess where we were. Jedder had a miner's lamp on his forehead and carried a twelve-bore gun. Aviston-Tresco had one arm in a sling and a lantern in his free hand. They were careless and confident, showing that Fosworthy was right and that they did not expect to have to deal with me.

They went on into the painted cave. If we had had any light, then was our chance to reach the entrance before they could. As it was, we were helpless. I was sure only of finding my way back to the wired passage, and that might well have taken ten minutes of patient concentration.

So far as we could tell, they were now examining the blocked entrance, where they must have been impressed by Fosworthy's burrowings. Aviston-Tresco still was calling. The wail of his voice through the black emptiness at last got on Fosworthy's nerves. He jumped to his feet before I could stop him and shouted:

"You can go to blazes, Tom! I'll get out of here yet!"

He sounded like a cocky schoolboy. He really was the most contradictory man. A pity that he ever had a fixed income behind which he could retire! If he had been compelled to come to terms with the world, he was as likely to have ended up as a mad mercenary in the Congo as a vegetarian in a country cottage.

They came running back, but it was impossible for them to fix the direction of the sound. I whispered to Fosworthy to lie still and shut up, reminding him of the gun under Jedder's arm. He apologized, far too loud, for forgetting his duty to protect me.

"We had better have the lights on," Jedder said.

He had arranged a relay system for this. He walked round the next corner and yelled "Light!" Far away I heard the call repeated. Then there was silence while some other helper presumably shouted the message back. The lights came on.

The pair did not attempt to look for Fosworthy. From their point of view, he might be anywhere — the maze of rock where he actually was or in some cleft or above or below them — and half a dozen strides would take him into darkness. Aviston-Tresco wanted, I believe, to avoid that, and was genuinely anxious that his former friend should dissolve without the long agony of starvation and blindness.

"There will be a meeting tonight, Barnabas," he said in a voice which would have been normal and inviting if the sinister echoes had not repeated it.

They retired slowly towards the changing room, carrying out some perfunctory searches on the way to look for my dead or prostrated body. I suspected that Jedder was not quite convinced that Aviston-Tresco had dealt with me successfully. He liked to have space and plenty of light around him and was continually turning round in case the unknown was following him. It was. We did in fact make some distance towards the entrance before the lights went out; but it was impossible to get ahead of the pair or to attack from behind.

Just in time we had passed the stretch of track with the foul drop on the right and were now in one of the finest caverns, high and with many openings, though most of them were dead ends. The only sane course was to stay exactly where we were till the time of the meeting. If we were not to exhaust ourselves looking for each other, we had to keep in actual, physical touch.

I asked Fosworthy what on earth Aviston-Tresco and that grim-faced brute Jedder were doing in his circle, some of whom would refuse to swat a mosquito. He accused me in his most academic tone of not paying attention to his precious synthesis and had another shot at it — now very much clearer since he was not distracted into mysticism by the presence of the paintings.

I will explain it very shortly at the risk of losing the metaphysical undertones. His unworldly, kindly little sect believed that all living things were individual radiations from a Whole and therefore equally worthy of respect. Yet they could not help seeing, being surrounded by a rural, traditional society, that the hunters of foxes, the fishers of trout and the shooters of game had a far more sympathetic understanding of animals than they.

Put it this way! If a tame fox could choose the most loving and generous boss for himself, he would certainly pick a Master of Fox Hounds, not a well-intentioned Fosworthy.

This, however, did not bother them so much as the paradox of Aviston-Tresco. All of them felt great admiration for him, yet his profession involved as much killing as healing. They were groping for the common ground between those who detested killing, those who had to do it and those who found it healthy and natural, when Jedder discovered the paintings. There were these ancestors of ours accepting that there was no difference between themselves and the animals, certain that the spirits of all continued to exist, yet killing to eat as steadily as any saber-toothed tiger.

So all of them arrived at the madly logical conclusion that since Life was one and survival unavoidable, killing was immaterial. But admittedly it caused pain and inconvenience. Therefore it must be carried out with formality and a request for forgiveness.

Absurd? Well, meet the eyes of any bird or animal which is dying by your hand! In the last throes the eyes, which at first were terrified, accept what is coming. I have never said "Forgive me!" but I recognize that I have wanted to. I cannot pretend to know, as those fanatics did, what the mammoth was thinking as its life drained out, but I am sure what that brilliantly perceptive artist and his fellow hunters were thinking.

I have no way of reconstructing the steps by which a vet, a handful of vegetarians and a few sportsmen came to find consolation in the same creed. Obviously they were all intensely religious in the sense that they wanted answers to unanswerable questions. Before I turned up, it had never occurred to Aviston-Tresco and Jedder that taking the life of a man was no different from taking that of an animal, but once they had convinced themselves that Fosworthy and I threatened their peace, it did occur to them.

"What caused the row?" I asked him.

"I told you. I wanted my woman. I said that what happens to love after dissolution was the only essential, that it was nonsense to talk of momentary inconvenience. A bird in the hand — if I may permit the vernacular to simplify my argument — is worth two in the bush. It was all so vital to me that I did, as Tom Aviston-Tresco said, threaten to make the controversy public and the cave too. I fear that sometimes my voice grows too excited. They thought I was out of my mind. People do, you know. I think you yourself were at first unsure of my sanity."

I was. But even this explanation did not wholly account for the persistence with which Fosworthy had been hunted down.

"And then I ran out," he went on, "with all of them shouting after me. Eventually they put me under restraint."

"Suppose Aviston-Tresco had caught you before you reached me, what would he have done?"

"Put me back."

"Where?"

"Here."

"You mean, you were held here? All alone?"

"Yes. Until I would give my word of honor to keep silent."

There at least they understood his character. It was unthinkable that so scrupulous a formalist would break his promise, even if given under duress.

"For how long?"

"It was very disturbing in the dark. Especially to a person of my temperament."

"How long do you think?" I repeated.

"Jedder cut off the light and took away my matches. It was not until I reached you that I found it had been only twenty-four hours. I must indeed have seemed to you distraught."

"And how did you get out in the end?"

"I am much afraid they drove me to violence when they came down to see if I were ready to surrender. As they were not expecting such behavior from me, it was temporarily successful. But not decisive. Aviston-Tresco was already halfway up the ladder behind me when I got out of the hatch."

So there at last was the full motive. It was not wholly because they wanted to protect the cave and to go on contemplating their discovery in peace. Above all they wanted to protect their precious selves, like most other criminals.

Those potentially dangerous people, as Dunton had called them, flared up at the very thought that their private chapel might be vulgarized and, to them, desecrated; then they were even more alarmed that Fosworthy might report what they, prominent and respectable local citizens, had done to him; and finally, when they were convinced that both their secret and their cruelty had come to the knowledge of a stranger who was only out to make money, at least two of them decided that dissolution — their gentle and fatuous euphemism — was the only way out.

We slept for some hours, huddled together to keep ourselves warm, and were awakened by the line of lamps. The big cavern where we were concealed was fairly well lit. Jedder, impressed by it, had at some time climbed up to fix two overhead lights. In contrast, the darkness of the holes was absolute. We found one which offered several ways of retreat.

They came in a trailing group through the cave, following the lighted passage. Aviston-Tresco was not with them. His exertions in the early morning must have been too much for his lacerated forearm. The appearance of the three men who led the way made it likely that they were sporting farmers, but they had not the tough, humorous faces of the breed. Though it may have been the hard light on high cheekbones, they seemed to me to have a common quality of cold, puritan self-discipline. I'd have trusted any of them where money was concerned, but run a mile from any contact with his private emotions. Then came the bank manager accompanied by a mild friend of the Fosworthy type with a thin, fair beard.

Miss Filk followed, a square and decisive Diana, leading two of her Dobermans. It said something for their training that they could negotiate the ladder. She made the casual group look like a procession, and I felt that her hounds would not be out of place in the painted cave. That seemed to be the lot, and I had high hopes of running for the entrance as soon as they had passed out of the cavern. Whatever Fosworthy said, the chap left in charge of the hatch and the switches was going to experience violence if I could get at him.

And then, behind the rest, came Jedder with Undine. She was well wrapped in a fur coat of her own. Her slender neck vanished into its illusory protection like a pencil of cascading water into rock. Impossible not to speculate on where it went. Difficult to accept the answer: nowhere. I must admit that in the underworld she was exquisite.

I could see that she had not been let into the secret before. The wonder and excitement in her face were genuine. Jedder and Aviston-Tresco had taken a chance that she would keep silent out of loyalty to Miss Filk or else they meant to give her a formal Apology later — in which case they might well have received one in return from her formidable protector.

It was hopeless. Fosworthy rushed away from me, grotesque as some emaciated ape from the depths of the limestone, hobbling on one foot with his filthy sheepskin flying behind him. His Dulcinea received him with her usual immaculate sweetness. She had clearly been warned that this was likely to happen. She knew from her own experience that he was wildly eccentric in spite of his strange charm, and she may have thought it a kindly act to trap him for his friends.

"You never told me you had joined us," he said. "I never knew."

"But you will come back with me?"

"It's quite all right, Barnabas," Jedder assured him.

He was in a daze of weakness, and in the presence of his Undine only capable of worship. I think that's the right word. I doubt if he formulated to himself precisely the tracing of those veins with hands and lips as that Midlands psychiatrist did. He was just certain that present and future were worthless without unspecified union with her. And now the outer world beckoned and

Jedder approved and she was willing to be escorted by him back to the light.

But even so he did not forget me. His chivalry, his self-imposed duty to protect me, came up against his infatuation and won.

"I would like, if I may, to accompany you all," he said.

I knew him well enough to see what he was up to. Whenever Fosworthy stopped to reflect, one could hear the wheels go round. He had calculated that if all the party went on peacefully towards the painted cave the way was clear for me to reach the hatch.

Jedder, too, hesitated. I don't know what instructions he had received from Aviston-Tresco or what he had in store for Fosworthy. The position was very tricky. All those people in the cave knew that Fosworthy had disappeared and why. But how had he returned? Possibly it had been explained to them that he had been found and was being held downstairs until other arrangements could be made. That was a good enough story for the milder souls who were appalled at the thought that he might impetuously publicize their secret but were quite incapable of murdering him.

Jedder had to make up his mind quickly. I am sure that the unexpected and convenient spot where Fosworthy had appeared made it up for him. He sent the others on, and allowed Fosworthy to follow with his enchantress. As soon as they had entered the passage which led out of the cavern, he ran after them. I was just about to get clear of my hidingplace when I saw him reach up and cut the loop of wire which turned the corner. At once and very silently he rushed up the familiar passage before anyone could recover from surprise and start feeling for matches or flashlights. Neither Fosworthy nor his girl had one. I heard the yell — of protest rather than terror — as Fosworthy went over the edge of the abyss, and Jedder shouting:

"Oh my God, he's slipped!"

There was nothing I could do. I was in absolute blackness. The whole party returned to the cavern. Some of them now had electric torches in hand, and I watched the beams and points of light flashing nervously all over the place, occasionally lighting a face, usually the lower part of a body. It was a world of shadows and unrecognizable half-humans. I shut my eyes against it and prayed that Fosworthy had been right and that he had in fact dissolved into an existence sunlit and forgiving, not into a hell without certainties such as he had left behind.

Undine was sobbing with shock.

"He was walking just outside me," she kept on saying. "Outside me to protect me from the drop."

"I tried to catch him as he slipped," Jedder insisted.

They yammered uncontrollably, and Miss Filk's dogs, catching the mood, began to bark. A voice remarked:

"We have to leave him there. It's better so."

"It will avoid questions," Jedder agreed. "And I promise you that only three of us know he was ever found."

I could bear it no longer. I was light-headed with fatigue and hunger and sorrow. If I had not relieved myself by some expression, I should have charged out and run amok.

"You bloody bastard!" I yelled.

There was panic. Nobody but Jedder knew anything at all of my existence. The beams searched all over the sweating walls which disguised sound. Two or three correctly pinpointed my position. I slid back unseen into the cleft behind me.

Jedder ordered them all back to the entrance at once, but Miss Filk stood her ground. She shouted in her most masculine manner:

"Who the devil is that?"

And then she let the two Dobermans off the leash and sicked them onto me. I heard them patter over the rocks and into my bolt-hole. There was no handy ledge up which to jump — and I should only have been treed there — but by a stroke of luck Miss Filk's flashlight as she charged after her savage brutes showed a loose rock.

I lifted it in both hands, like former inhabitants of the cave, and crashed it down on the head of the first dog as he sank his teeth into my shielding coat. The other ran away, howling. It was an uncanny place in which to ask a dog to attack, especially when the eyes of the hunted had acquired mysterious night sight if any light at all was reflected from the glazed walls of the cave.

Miss Filk caught the contagion of terror from her remaining dog and tied herself up among the rocks. She was quite correct in thinking I was close behind her. I badly needed her torch. I doubt if she even knew how she lost it. Her screams brought up some dim figures to collect her who were furiously attacked by the Doberman. Her efforts to control it restored her normally firm character.

I saw their lights disappear on the way to the entrance. I could, I suppose, have chased and haunted the lot of them until they were incapable with fear. But I was on my last legs and in no condition to meet a determined Jedder who knew only too well what my physical weakness must be even if I had survived Aviston-Tresco's attentions.

So I went back to the recess for the body of the dog and put it across my shoulders, hanging onto the four legs. That collapsed me in a few strides. My civilized intention was to cook the meat, but nature was insistent. Lying there with my head on the warm body and a better blade in my pocket than the flints of the cave painters I lapped back my life as they would have lapped.

I lay there in the empty silence. How long I do not know. It must have been hours, for I became very thirsty and the dog was stiffening. I remember whimpering with self-pity as I started for the entrance by the light of Miss Filk's torch, dragging the carcass behind me. It puzzled me that I had succeeded in lifting it to my shoulders. I must have been compelled by some obsession in my exhausted mind that lifting was the right way. An influence of the hunters, perhaps.

The torch began to fade and glow pink. I stumbled about in a frantic search for paraffin, by the light of matches which I had noticed with the lanterns in the changing room. At last I found a full five-gallon can under the steps, filled a lantern and lit it. That was about the only moment of relief, almost of content, which I had known since I was unloaded into the barn upstairs.

There were some pit-props in the tool store, so I built a fire on the spot and half grilled Doberman chops over a couple of iron crowbars. They tasted delicious. Two days later, when my hunger was appeased, they tasted utterly foul and I had to force myself to eat them.

Days, I say; but of course there weren't any. My watch kept ticking, and I cut a notch on the changing-room table for every period of twelve hours. From then on I had an accurate record of the passing of time.

One thing was certain: that nobody would return to the cave until positive that I was dead. They might or might not think of the saving carcass. I reckoned that it would never occur to them. However that might be, I had to face my loneliness for at least a week and probably more. I think now that I should have spotted the solution, although it would have been no earthly use to me since I had not the strength. The long, cool, work-manlike job would have become a mere hysterical tearing at brickwork followed by collapse.

But endurance I had. I put it down to being an engineer with experience of deep mines, for I have no exceptional force of character, only an obstinate desire to live. I refused to spend my time just sitting. I had to find myself things to do. After taking care that there was nothing in the changing room or gallery which could reveal my presence at a glance, I chose for my headquarters an alcove some way along the passage, but near enough for me to hear any sound from the entrance. Well inside the cave, the air felt fresher than at the dead end. I was afraid that my fire, always glowing but seldom built up unless shivering became intolerable, might use up too much oxygen. It was my source of light as well as comfort. I never lit a lantern unless at work.

I was in two minds whether to mend the lighting system or not, dreading the disappointment when the storage batteries ran down. Of course I could not in the end resist the temptation. I found the break, repaired it and replaced the fuse. Nothing happened. The batteries were dead. Before leaving the changing room Jedder had short-circuited the lot. It was another sign of his determination to finish with me.

Though I dared not move far from the track of the wired passage for fear of losing myself, I found an occupation in exploring details of geology. I was able to reconstruct a lot more of the story than Fosworthy had told me. Jedder had brilliantly used compass and measuring rods — his naval training — and established that an upward sloping pothole must be nearly under his barn. When he and his friends, after the discovery of the paintings, went to work on it, they drove a rock drill up to the surface and found that Jedder's dead reckoning was wrong by only about thirty yards. It was then easy to dig the shored gallery through broken rock and earth, and burrow straight up into the barn.

Often I returned to the painted cave, finding more and more in it. A lantern — better still, two lanterns —

gave to the beasts more beauty and mystery than Jedder's too naval lighting.

I had lively company there, for I plotted and analyzed the movements of the conventionally drawn little men. It was like contemplating some spirited wallpaper when half awake; one sees designs of which the artist was hardly conscious. I came to know that group of families which had hunted its way up from the Mediterranean following the game to the colder rivers and the young forests. The paintings must have been made during a short interglacial. The ice cap over Britain stopped short of the Mendips, but would have made the climate too harsh for Paleolithic hunters. Hot sun must be assumed and the conditions, say, of a high Swiss valley in summer.

The ritual of the Apology was plain as could be. And the mammoth deserved it. I could sense their respect for so rare and magnificent a source of meat with a spirit inside it. Could it have been a first arrival as the trees withered and the tundra began, or a last survivor as the interglacial brought up the warmth and the southern hunters?

I think I came nearer to emotional understanding of the effect which the paintings had on Fosworthy. In utter loneliness one begins to remember not only facts but one's former memories of the facts. My train of thought started with a hungry night in the forests of Honduras. The two Indians with me caught a fat iguana. By the light of our fire I watched it killed, cut up and grilled. Nothing surprising in that. Any country boy has done the same to a rabbit.

But when, back in a modern city, I thought of this slow, pathetic and very welcome lizard I was astonished that the scene in memory seemed to me to have a deeper and purer significance than the mere filling of a belly. In that is a faint reflection of Fosworthy's synthesis. To him the frigid inhumanity of the butcher's shop and the slaughterhouse was revolting. So was the taking of life for sport. Like the vast majority of mankind in industrial civilization, he had never killed in order to live. Even his imagination could not conceive the possibility. It took the paintings to reveal to him that the hunter experienced not only the sympathy with the animal which we all know, but an enrichment of the spirit which we have utterly lost.

Religion was very present in so after-death a place with its single, concentrated glory of art. Though I am not much of a Christian, I have carried for years my King James Bible and know much of it by heart as our grandfathers did. If it is not inspired, then what does inspiration mean? I do not, of course, refer to its historical accuracy or literal truth, but just to its superb language. It was great consolation to me to remember *Out of the depths have I cried unto thee, O Lord,* though I have no more conception of what I was crying to than the mammoth in the moment of death. Fosworthy would have said that it did not matter, and I doubt if it does.

These journeys of mine around my tomb, pointless except for keeping up morale, were safe enough while it was day outside. Fosworthy had told me that his people only made their occasional visits in the late evening when all the fields were empty, to avoid attracting attention. The difference between day and night I knew from my twelve-hour notches on the table. So, towards what would be sunset, I came home to my alcove or the changing room and remained there.

Trying to foresee the actual circumstances of my escape, I had to recognize that I should have more than Jedder and his twelve-bore to deal with and that I could expect no mercy. I think few of the sect would ever have agreed to remove me merely because of my knowledge of the cave; but now I was a witness to the death of Fosworthy and the attempted murder of myself by starvation, to which they were all accessories. Frightened men, able at a pinch to find justification for conscience, would come prepared to finish me off discreetly in case, against all expectations, I were alive.

To escape was going to be desperately difficult if their routine was always to leave a man at the top of the shaft; and it was prudent to reckon on at least one more on guard in or about the changing room while the rest hunted far and wide for me or my body.

Against all this opposition I had to go up the ship's companion, along the narrow, earth-cut gallery, up the aluminum ladder and through the hatch. One armed man could stop me anywhere. If he failed, his colleague in the barn had only to pull up the ladder, and there I was.

In the darkness I made vivid pictures of the action to come and forced my imagination to take them slowly and sanely. I saw that I had to create such confusion that everyone would be occupied sorting it out, and the man on top would rush down to lend a hand.

I sawed one of the steps of the companion ladder nearly through on the under side. Whoever stepped on it would crash down with his full weight on the hinder edge of the step below. On this edge I did some inlay work with detonators from the tool store — ten of them set an inch apart. I tried one out in a small cavity. A flat stone weighing about a pound, dropped from a height of two feet, set it off.

The heavy tools available were designed for shoring, not marquetry, so my booby trap was a clumsy job. Still, it could not possibly be detected by a man coming down the steps. Some sort of spectacular accident was bound to happen. I hoped it would happen soon, for the end of the paraffin was in sight and I was down to making soup of Doberman bones. A sinewy bitch she was, with little meat on her. I would have done better out of the fine glossy beast which had visited my flat.

On the twelfth evening after Fosworthy's death I heard some dull sound which was not the last echo of a distant fall of rock. I went up the companion ladder — with considerable care — and into the dug gallery. Feet were trampling at the top of the vertical shaft as the hay bales were removed from the hatch.

That the crisis had at last arrived bewildered me. I had become too accustomed to blindness, silence and withdrawal. Shaking all over, certain that I was going to die, I went into the tool store and chose a crowbar. I was quite incapable of making any more plans. I simply stood in the passage outside the changing room, still trembling, and put out my lantern. All postions seemed equally objectless. A sound instinct. What was going to matter were their movements, not mine.

I heard the aluminum ladder go through the hatch and down. A whole platoon of feet, as it seemed to me, scuffled over the rubble of the gallery, and the leader began to descend the companion. There was an almighty crash as the sawn step gave way, but no explosion. The new arrival had somehow managed to miss the step below and the hand rail as well. He yelled:

"God! This thing's rotted, Alan! I might have broken my leg."

He must have picked up the fallen plank and placed it on the step below, on top of the detonators. A tidy fellow! Or perhaps he was so shaken and annoyed that he wanted to show up Jedder then and there as a lousy carpenter. He was very lucky not to have set off the detonators. Standing below the companion, his face and eyes were on a level with the mined step.

The next man, who turned out to be Jedder, came running down and took one flying stride over the gap. There was a flash which hurt my eyes, a report which sounded almost shrill, then a rumbling of echoes mixed up with the slither and thud of the falling body. I was afraid that the whole companion ladder had gone, though I knew well that the effect of the detonators must be local.

Someone else following behind screamed: "His foot! Come!"

I let them come. What I had planned in the darkness

had happened; and this reality, this hope of the sun, changed me from hunted into hunter. On hands and knees I felt my way round the cold corner of rock at the entrance to the changing room and looked in. I need not have taken such precautions. There was a dim group of three around Jedder. A fifth person was up in the gallery asking if he could help. They told him to go back to the barn.

They were very careless. After all, they could hardly be expected to think of anything but the unconscious Jedder who had been stunned by the shock and his fall. The sawn step laid on top of the detonators had saved his foot from being blown to bits, but it was hedge-hogged with splinters of teak and scraps of copper, and bleeding profusely. Every flashlight was directed at him.

One obvious gun — unreachable — was leaning against what was left of the companion; a dark line, which could be another, was on the ground. I wriggled towards it and closed my hand on the smooth wood of a stock. Even if someone had looked up, I should have been invisible to his eyes.

As I broke the gun open to see that it was loaded, one of them heard me. I daresay he also heard the click of the safety catch. Two beams of light were concentrated on me.

I told them to come out from under the companion and stand with faces to the rock wall, hands raised. Having collected one of the dropped torches glimmer-ing on the floor and stamped on the rest, I made them a very formal Apology, trusting that when they were dissolved they would realize that this was necessary and that I bore no malice. One of them fainted. The other two pressed themselves into the limestone as if they hoped to go through it, farther away from me.

This was sheer, satisfying cruelty, for I knew I could not kill in cold blood and never intended to. While they waited for death, I collected the second gun and swarmed up the outer edge and rail of the companion. I wasn't out of the wood yet and I knew it. The fellow who had been ordered back to his post must surely have stopped to listen to what was going on. I arrived at the foot of the aluminum ladder just in time to see it disappear through the open hatch.

He did not put his head over the edge of the shaft. An unnecessary precaution. The man in control of that ladder was the last person on earth I would have shot.

"I will not let you out before the rest of them," he said.

I tried hard to appear reasonable and told him that it was hardly likely that I would wait to be last.

"In any case they can't move," I added, "because they haven't any light."

If I really believed that, I was quite wrong. Even in pitch darkness it was not difficult to climb the companion and crawl along the gallery.

I heard my cracked, unfamiliar voice warning him that if he did not drop the ladder I would go back and execute his friends one by one. He was not impressed.

"Then I should close up the hatch and you would die with them," he said primly.

I recognized his style. He was that wretched bank

manager. He was terrified, but it was still second nature to bargain with a client.

"If you don't let me out, Jedder will bleed to death."

That didn't seem to me much of an argument, but it made him hesitate.

"What are your minimum requirements?" he asked, as if not prepared to go far on such dubious security.

"You will drop the ladder and come down it."

"I will not! I will not!" he bleated. Naturally enough, he was not going to risk being shut up forever with his friends. "I shall go and fetch the police."

"Like hell you will! And stand trial for murder? But if you let me out I shall allow you to telephone for an ambulance."

"I cannot explain."

"If you all tell the same lie, you can," I answered, without any serious thought that this might indeed be true and very dangerous for my future. "You will have time to shut up the cave."

A voice boomed along the gallery: "Don't let him out! Don't let him out!"

My beam of light showed nothing but the yellow walls of the tunnel and its unsteady shoring. The speaker must have put his head up and bobbed down again.

"Then listen to what I am going to do!" I said. "They have no light down there. I have smashed their torches. I shall drive them far into the cave and leave them there. Only you can get them out."

The hatch slammed shut for an answer, cutting off the very dim circle of light in which I stood.

Their moves seemed to me panic-stricken, leading nowhere. I felt for the second gun, which was on the ground, unloaded it and pocketed the two cartridges. Then I stood on the barrel and bent it. If I could not get out, nobody else was going to.

I was not very intelligent. It could hardly be expected of a man who was insane with longing for light and human society. A contradictory set of responses. I would have torn that bank manager to pieces if it was likely to do any good. Yet at the same time, because he talked to me, I could have embraced him with tears. Not a mood in which to deal with the unexpected. They may have calculated on it. They had had time to think.

I went back along the gallery to the top of the companion and shone my torch down into the changing room. It was empty. The three men, carrying Jedder, seemed already to have retired into the darkness where I proposed to drive them. I did not see what they were going to gain by that and started down the companion. A crowbar slung with an underhand action whirled past my face and clanged against the rock.

Snapping off my light, I jumped back to safety in the gallery. So that was it. They were prepared to fight it out, three against one in the darkness — and such complete darkness that my trained night sight did not count. I had no heart for anything of the sort. All my little store of nervous energy had been exhausted by the explosion and its sequel. I simply wanted to get out of that awful place and I nearly scurried like a rabbit back to the end of my burrow below the hatch.

But it was no good retreating to a pointless safety.

Unless the ladder came down, I was trapped; and it was impossible to guess when or for what cause it would come down. The bank manager would presumably have to open the hatch from time to time to hear what was going on and to receive orders, if any. Or he might close it up and replace the hay bales when day returned outside.

Were they prepared to stick it out for twenty-four hours if necessary? Looking back on it, I don't see how they could. Five persons missing from their farms or businesses would surely have been reported to the police. As it was, however, I could only think they were prepared to stay down, and was consumed by impotent fury and impatience. On that, too, they may have counted. They were far from fools except in the matter of their blasted metaphysical animism.

All of this was felt rather than reasoned out. I remember two things only were clear: that the rabbit might be a rabbit but had no more patience; and that they had everything to gain, all problems solved, by sending my body to join Fosworthy's, whereas I was no better off if I killed them.

So I scrambled down the companion without showing a light. They had another shot at the noise with a hammer and hit the rail. With such deadly accurate throwing-in one of them could have played cricket for Somerset. Obviously he was in the passage outside the changing room, popping in and out of the entrance. My gun was not much use, though I had a cartridge for each of the three and one over for Jedder if he asked for it. I placed the flashlight under the barrels so that I could hold the lot in my left hand with thumb on the switch. A clumsy arrangement. I saw a head once, but it wasn't there by the time the gun was up to my shoulder.

Feeling my way silently into the passage, I tiptoed along the wall of the cave, hoping that I was driving them all in front of me and that the gun barrels would soon touch something soft. It was soon clear that I was wrong. After I sent a quick beam ahead of me, another lump of iron came at me from behind. I jumped round and fired. The flash showed my attacker only a few yards away. I missed him by miles but got a gasping yelp out of him. Probably shot had ricocheted off the rock face and stung him up.

I had one in front of me and one behind. The third had to be in the changing room or the tool store. They had worked it out well. Whichever I hunted, there was always another ready to dash in on the quick flash of the torch. It seems to me now that I should have had it all my own way since I was armed and they were not; but in fact one of them had only to creep or dodge within reach, and then whatever weapon he had found among Jedder's stores was more efficient than four feet of gun pointing the wrong way. Admittedly if it happened to be pointing the right way one of them was going to experience the unity of life in the happy hunting grounds.

I still liked the plan with which I had impulsively threatened the bank manager — of shepherding all of them in front of me into convolutions of darkness from which they could never escape without a light. Thinking about it — if it can be called thinking — I saw that

I was being far too cautious. Since by now I knew the wired passage as a blind man knows his living room, I could always move a little faster than they could. So I concentrated on the man ahead of me, cracking on the pace and no longer bothering about the noise I made.

I could not catch him, but he had to stumble away into nothingness a lot more recklessly than he liked. He passed the alcove with the still glowing ashes of my last fire and began to run, realizing that I might be able to see him. I did just distinguish a hurrying shadow, but it was not worth wasting a shot. The job was done. I heard him tripping and panting. I heard him fall, pick himself up and patter on again. I kept up the pressure until I was fairly sure that he had taken a wrong turning. If he hadn't, he was going to in the very near future.

I turned round and made for the changing room, moving more cautiously. The man who had threatened my back and was now ahead of me had been outdistanced. It was some minutes before I heard his retreating footsteps. I stopped to listen but all was silent. He had arrived wherever he wanted to be.

There were three possible places: the changing room, the tool store or the dead end between them. First I made certain that the dead end was clear. I had to pass both entrances, which I did by approaching silently and then rushing them. Even with my perfect knowledge of every twist and obstacle I still managed to slam my shoulder against rock. Once at the end I had command of the situation and could return to the attack with torch and gun barrels pointing in the right direction, sure that no one was behind me.

I crawled into the changing room, convinced that I must be heard and had better keep low. But there was no loose stone or patch of mud to give me away. Everything was silent. Everybody was listening. I got my back against the wall where I was safe from any of the cricketer's missiles, stood up and swept the little cave with gun barrels and light.

No. 2 was there, defenseless except for a hammer. Without saying a word, I beckoned him towards me, then jumped behind him and stuck the gun in his back. There was no need for any light. I prodded him on ahead of me into the passage and into the tool store, where I knew No. 3 must be. He was. He hurled himself at the entrance, thinking that the approaching steps were mine, and doubled up No. 2 with a knee which landed in the groin and a flying fist which hit limestone. I took a kick at the mess in passing and stood back. They cannot have seen much of me, but the lighted barrels were unmistakable.

That was the end. I stripped them of matches and lighters and made them march ahead of me up the passage and into the great cavern where Undine had innocently pulled her Delilah on Fosworthy. Just before we got there, No. 1 came running to the light shouting "Thank God!" His thanks were cut short and he joined the procession.

When I had them in the middle of the cavern, I suddenly turned off the light and started to hit out in all directions with the butt of the gun. That effectively scattered them. In fact they ran farther than was necessary. I suspect that they were taking the opportunity to dive into cover. I doubt if they foresaw at all what was going to happen to them.

Since entering the great cave I had been carefully counting my steps, for I knew well that I could not take liberties with the place as soon as my torch was switched off. I about-turned very exactly, risked one flash to be sure that my feet were pointing in the right direction and tiptoed off. Even so I did not expect to hit the entrance. Experience in the dark had taught me that I always bore a little left. So, when the counted steps led me nowhere, I turned sharp right and — still with some anxiety — came to an angle of the rock wall. Once round the corner I could safely give myself light, and was soon back in the tool store.

Jedder was lying in a corner, well out of the way of any trouble, with a sheepskin coat under him. When I was rounding up his two friends, my eye had been caught by the white bandage which had been twisted round his leg below the knee, but I had no time to investigate.

His eyes were open. He stared without saying anything while I lit a lantern. I think my filthy and savage appearance haunted him more than the fear of what I might do. I was a living corpse. I had no right to be alive.

"You have — you have been down with Fosworthy?" he asked.

"No. Not poor Fosworthy. Doberman."

He gave a sigh of relief, or perhaps merely of regret that he had never remembered the dog.

"You and I are alone," I said. "Your friends are lost."

"Nonsense!" he replied. "It's not all that bad."

An unimaginative man. Evidently he had never explored without a light in his hand and a line behind him.

"You are going to shout to that bank manager to lower the ladder."

"Why should I?"

"Because if you don't, you will be begging for death before I've done with you."

"I will not let you out."

I regret what I did. It would not have been necessary to anyone who was less obtuse.

He had very little feeling in his leg below the tourniquet but plenty above. For a moment I could not think of any tortures. One needs to know the technique of these things, and one needs fire. Then I remembered that some Jedder-like character in history used to flay his political enemies alive with red-hot pincers. There may be some point in the heat. I found even a thin strip very difficult with cold pincers.

He agreed to shout for help, moaning in self-pity that he could not believe one human being would do that to another. Curious. I should have thought that shutting a man up in the dark to die of starvation was more vile — though less spectacular a crime — than ribboning his skin. But I didn't argue. We had to get on. He might be right in assuming that his three companions could return.

I untied his hands and put him on my back. It was not easy to hoist him up the companion, but there again experience counted. I had done this before in my career — many times in practice and once in earnest when I had been just as weak from smoke as I now was from hunger. He complicated the lift by making a grab for the gun which I was foolishly trying to carry as well. I had no mercy on him after that. I dragged him along the gallery by his good leg, leaving myself a hand free.

When we were crouching below the hatch I told him to shout. He seemed unwilling. So I had to point out again that, though we both knew I could not kill him, I was prepared to go on working over him until there was nothing left but a voice.

He shouted all right at the first touch, but it did no good whatever. The bank manager may have replaced some of the hay and deadened sound. More probably he was in such a state of panic that he had left the barn and was skulking outside, all ready to bolt for safety if any stranger came along.

"You've got me, I know it," Jedder gasped in the silence. "But listen to me! You have to keep quiet about all this. For God's sake, don't you see it?"

I told him to explain quickly what he meant, and that it was no use wasting time. If his friends got clear and came crawling along the gallery I should shoot them down without mercy.

"I mean that if you go to the police, you will find yourself charged with the murder of Barnabas Fosworthy."

I told him to go to hell, that it was no good trying to

bluff me with such damned idiocy and that anyway Miss Carlis knew how Fosworthy died.

"She thought he slipped until you terrified her," he answered. "And then her good Filk gibbering with hysteria! She likes to think that what killed Fosworthy wasn't human. A thing! She doesn't know it was you. She's a shallow fool. You'd know it if you had ever met her."

So they were not aware that I had. That could be useful, and worth exploring further.

"Fosworthy confided in me that he intended to meet her at the Pavilion Hotel," I said. "What was she told when he never turned up?"

It suited his game to answer, and the story was credible. It all came pouring out between spasms of pain while I kept the beam of the torch on his nervously working face.

Miss Filk appeared at the hotel later that day and tried to patch up the quarrel. She explained to her Cynthia that Fosworthy had fits of believing that he had enemies and that his only safety was in disappearing. A very common delusion. I myself had at first wondered if that was his trouble.

Undine was not convinced and returned to Bath. Miss Filk kept after her. Her need for the wretched girl's friendship overcame discretion. She told her that Fosworthy's mind had given way completely, that he had gone down a cave and would not come out. This infuriated Jedder and Aviston-Tresco, but they had to submit to Miss Filk. She was too dangerous and unpredictable. She insisted that her ward should see Fosworthy and be cured of her interest in him. She knew that he would appear insane after days alone in the darkness, even if he was not.

"And my motive for murdering Fosworthy?" I asked, returning to the main point.

"That's for the police to say when they find his body. Accounts will prove you bribed him. What for, if not to show you the cave? Aviston-Tresco and I tried to interfere but were brutally attacked by you. We were all alarmed at the thought of you and Fosworthy underground together — one of you unbalanced and the other violent. So we came down to the rescue. We found neither of you."

"Why didn't you report it? "

"We thought you had both left. It was only when we came back after twelve days that we suspected you had killed him. And you then tried to kill us."

"It won't stand up for a moment," I said.

"Are you sure? While you've been away —" I could have torn him apart for that "away" — "Aviston-Tresco's arm has been amputated. Then you blew me up with a land-mine. You can't deny either. Won't that suggest to a jury that you stick at nothing? If you talk, Yarrow, you're in for a difficult case in which the evidence of respectable local citizens will be stacked against you. You and your counsel may convince the jury that your story is true and ours is invented, but is it worth the gamble? Is it worth awaiting trial in jail? So dangerous a man will not get bail."

I was not up to arguing. It was highly unlikely that I could not get the lot of them convicted. On the other hand it was true enough that I should be in for many unpleasant and anxious months.

"So you will leave me alone if I leave you alone?"

"Of course! Why should we start anything up? I don't want all the scandal and fifteen years in jail at the end of it."

From my unrevealing darkness I replied that I should do my best to get it for him and that I was not going to spend the next year or two looking over my shoulder. Their interest in my death was too strong. It would solve all their problems.

"For God's sake, we're a small band of harmless countrymen or were till you turned up!" he exclaimed. "We're not assassins trained to take risks. A bungled attempt on you would be the end of us. You are quite safe so long as we are."

I agreed to think it over, but refused to give my word. "I don't want . . ."

His face had gone dead white. That he had been able to force out so many words before collapse impressed me with his argument, perhaps too strongly. He pulled himself back from unconsciousness for a last retort:

"I don't want your word, damn you!"

I never worked with more anxiety to bring anyone round. I went back to the changing room to get a coat, and packed him in that and my own. No sugar, hot tea or alcohol. Nothing but water colder than he was. As a last resort I loosened the bandage above his knee and let him bleed a bit. To my surprise that worked. He opened his eyes and murmured:

"I shall not dissolve. He's bound . . . to open up . . . soon."

It was all of an hour before very cautiously he did.

I raved at the bank manager that his friends were lost in the darkness and that Jedder would die if he couldn't get help quick. He threw the hatch wide open, shone a torch down the shaft and saw that I was telling the truth.

"Drop that ladder at once, you fool!"

This only reduced him to dithering.

"I don't know what to do," he wailed, more to himself than to me. "I don't know what to do. All this! It will be the end of me."

I heard him pacing round the rim of the open hatch, and stop suddenly as if he had forced himself to a decision.

"I won't come down until you are out," he said.

I had to accept that, though I was suspicious. The ladder came down far too readily, all in a nervous rush which nearly landed the foot of it on Jedder. Had it occurred to him that when my head came up to ground level I should be at his mercy? Well, if it had, there was little I could do about it. I could only trust to his character. He was a peaceable, very white-collared citizen, needing his office chair to make decisions. His fear of the law and of insecurity was desperate enough to screw him up to hit, but he was sure to do it inefficiently. The game was to play on his nerves.

I climbed within two feet of the top and stopped to listen. He, too, was silent, which again suggested that I shouldn't trust him. We had arrived at another impasse. He could not now withdraw the ladder, but he could, if I tried him too hard, slam down the hatch on the top of it. His somewhat bronchial breathing revealed that he was waiting for me near the edge behind the ladder, where the back of my head would come into sight first.

Naturally I had taken the gun with me. Quickly raising it in one hand so that the barrels were just in the open and the butt against the wall of the shaft, I fired. Of course I missed him, but probably not by much. In any case this was altogether too brutal a business for him. I shot out of the hatch, and there he was crouching in the hay, trying to disassociate himself from the huge beam of wood at his side. I cannot believe that he could ever have raised and dropped it in time. Perhaps he meant to swing it at me like a battering ram.

I had no use for him at all. I ordered him to get his friends out first, and then telephone for an ambulance. This was quite instinctive and showed that for the moment I had accepted Jedder's proposal. I wanted them to have the hay bales back on the hatch and Jedder laid out on the floor of the barn before public authorities arrived. What story they told was their own business.

The key was in the door. When I had turned it and was out on the open hills, I felt relief too overwhelming for anger or revenge. The night sky, intolerably welcome, was dark blue to my eyes, and the red and white of the stars were vivid as candles on a Christmas tree.

I trotted away between the shadowy barrows of the dead and over the springing turf of the sheep lands on much the same route that Fosworthy must have taken when he was just a jump ahead of Aviston-Tresco. Remembering his appearance, I stopped somewhere above The Green Man and its hamlet wondering what I in my turn must look like. I had never gone to the trouble of hanging up a lantern in the changing room to find out. The inside of me was alarming enough without bothering about the outside.

My unthinking intention had been to take the first available public transport back to London. That now seemed unwise. Whether Jedder was dead or alive, his injuries were curious enough to interest the police, however firmly his friends stuck to an improbable story. Suspicious characters — and I certainly was that — were likely to be asked to account for themselves.

So I could not reach London as I was, nor did The Green Man offer safety. Well-disposed though the Gorms were, I was not capable of inventing a story which would explain my appearance. The only possible friend to whom I could go was Dr. Dunton. He would be inclined to believe me, since he knew something of the human background.

His house was down in the plain, only five miles off across the valley as the crow flies. But I was no crow. As soon as I started to stumble down the steep escarpment I was overcome by exhaustion, tripping over obstacles which, when I looked at them, were barely visible. The gray dawn showed a melancholy field of wheat surrounded by gray dry-stone walls. I crawled into it.

When I woke, the sun was well up and breakfast of a sort was all round me. I rubbed the ears of wheat between my hands and licked up the little piles of kernels.

Perhaps I was not so hungry as I thought, or else I kept closing my eyes against the sun which hurt them. However it was, I went fast asleep again.

In the afternoon I was sharply waked up by a dog which jumped the wall, raced barking towards me and then retreated cautiously to its master — who had stopped alarmingly near — pretending a mistake had been made. Its nose may have distinguished at close quarters what my recent diet had been. I was uneasy at setting up a presumption of guilt by being discovered in hiding, and decided that there was no object in hanging about till nightfall. The best bet was to strike straight across country while I could see where I was going and to reach Dunton's house soon after dusk. I was probably right. The easier route was round by the road through nearly linked villages and the outskirts of Wells, but at that time of year, even after dark, it was far too public.

North of Westbury I slipped across the Cheddar road, crossed the railway and was soon in trouble on Westbury Moor. Seen from the hillside, the fields and hedges of the rich valley looked easily passable. I ought to have noticed the willows. There was not a hedge without a stream beneath it or a field which was not cut by a deep drain. It was as bad as being tied up in irrigated paddy fields. Movement would have been simpler in the Dark Ages when the damned place was an estuary instead of splendid pasture at nearly sea level. At high tide Arthur and the mourning women could have sailed straight off from Glastonbury to the Western Isles.

So I had to wade to a causeway and follow the little

lane on top of it. I could not help being conspicuous. A farm tractor chugged past me and nearly stopped, but the driver thought better of it. Some children took one look and bogged themselves to the knees in their anxiety to get off the track and away from me.

This forced me to take more serious stock of myself. I had a fortnight's growth of beard, matted with filth. The bruise on my jaw had gone down, but beneath it was a jagged wound in the neck which, my fingers told me, had healed at the bottom and was still open at the top. It was leaking a little and must have looked disgusting. I couldn't hide it, for the buttons had gone from my shirt. The state of the collar was, anyway, worse.

My appearance was more forbidding than I had ever realized. My clothes were not torn as badly as Fosworthy's, but were stiff with a cement of limestone dust, earth from the gallery, and blood — streaks of mine down the front of my coat, streaks of Doberman's down the back and spots of Jedder's. From the knees down, I was soggy with the black mud of the ditches.

And now there was a second main road which had to be crossed with no chance of avoiding people and houses. My lane led me slap into the village of Henton. Since I could not get round it without swimming, I elected to make a dash for the telephone box and ask Dunton to drive out and pick me up. Then I found that I had not got four pennies. Pound notes, yes. But all loose change had fallen out of my pockets when I was upside down or collapsed.

Who the hell ever has four pennies except a salesman prepared for telephoning? If you want to telephone in this island you must first go into a shop and get change. Buy something for twopence — if you can think of anything which only costs twopence — offer sixpence, ask for pennies and not the halfpennies you are sure to be offered, and then find a public box in working order. For the returned exile or the foreign visitor it is easier to back a horse than to telephone.

While I hesitated, a man strode briskly round the corner towards me. He had a mass of windblown white hair and an ash plant for a walking stick. I could not avoid him and summed him up as best I could. He seemed to be one of the mild, exaggeratedly healthy people by whom that part of the county was infested. At a guess, retired and sixtyish, though appearing in his late forties. Probably a militant atheist or devoted to some local religion. But on that point I was prejudiced.

I hoped that he would take me for a singularly disreputable tramp and pass by. But tramps are no longer recognized as a normal and picturesque decoration of the countryside. The very few who wander from place to place do so from choice rather than necessity and are well enough dressed to pick up a lift if they want it.

He stopped and wished me good evening.

"You shouldn't be walking in that condition," he said with severe benevolence.

"I know I shouldn't. Can you give me four pennies to telephone with?"

"Haven't got them," he replied, "but we will get

change in the village. You should have that wound attended to immediately. I am afraid you have been fighting."

There was a Fosworthian echo in that. I did not want him to disapprove of me, since he might be useful, so I said impulsively that I had been in a car accident.

"An accident? When?"

"About a week ago."

As soon as the words were out of my mouth, I realized the mistake. My appearance was quite consistent with being hurled out onto a very dirty road. But what had I been doing ever since and why had nobody patched me up?

"Come with me, my dear chap!" he urged. "This must be looked into. I am sure you have no reason to be alarmed."

There was nothing else for it. I walked slowly towards the village with him. It was not difficult to drag my feet and play even tireder than I felt. He offered to leave me where I was and telephone for me.

What was I to do? I was not going to give him my name and have it officiously batted about the district, and I would not drag Dunton and his family publicly into my affairs. He had too much to lose if things went wrong.

I asked this unreliable altruist if he had a car. He replied fussily that he had never found any necessity for one. This confirmed my instinctive guess that he was a devoted pedestrian and about to tell the nearest policeman that there was a wandering man who had

been knocked senseless and had probably killed someone else into the bargain.

In my condition the complications were beyond me. I
gave him an imaginary telephone number, and then sat
down on the edge of the drain and let him carry on. As
soon as he was safely out of sight, I waded across to the
meadow, found no cover, waded another ditch into
somebody's orchard and took refuge in the branches of
an apple tree. I was very wet and cold, but beyond caring. I found some comfort in the green of the mass of
leaves and the red of a clear sunset down the valley. I
still could not take light for granted.

After twenty minutes my old hearty returned, beat
about a little and shouted "Hi!" A little later a cop arrived on a motorcycle. Neither of them thought of looking for me on the other side of the water. They assumed
that I had gone back up the lane and could easily be
overtaken. The walker continued his walk, fuming a little and waving his ash plant impatiently. The cop shot
off towards Westbury.

I proposed to let twilight deepen before I moved. Sitting in my tree, I cursed myself for a coward who preferred to be hunted by police rather than go boldly to
them with my story. Yet it was undeniable that life, as
soon as it became recognizable, would be easier and
pleasanter if I could manage to clear out and leave no
trace of my existence. Suppose they did gang up and
swear I killed Fosworthy? Suppose the hospital, picking
bits of teak and detonator out of Jedder, started asking
how an explosion could peel off a neat ribbon of skin?

Whoever went on trial in the end, I was in for a packet of trouble. I had no intransigent desire to bring them all to justice. They were the least likely people in the world to repeat their crime. And anyway rough justice had been done.

For God's sake get out of here! was all I could say to myself, but I knew I was not capable of any prolonged physical effort. I had to steal something to eat, since I could not buy it without attracting pity and questions. A likely spot was a large lowland farm with extensive outbuildings close to the point where I had disentangled myself from the drains of Westbury Moor.

I went back up the lane, and approached the house upwind. It was blazing with light behind curtains and there was not a soul in the yard. An old, half-boarded window opening which faced the marshland gave access to a building in which were a couple of sows about to farrow. Their quarters, so far as I could tell by feeling about, were far too clean and scientific. No edible scraps had been left to rot.

I let myself out into the yard and looked for the cowshed. Either there wasn't one or I couldn't find it. I came across two battery houses for hens, but both were locked. The farmer did not eat battery eggs himself, however, for I disturbed a few chickens roosting on the tractors and machinery in an open Dutch barn. I searched all likely crannies and corners in the hope of discovering where they laid — hard enough in daylight — and eventually came upon two eggs in the chaff at the bottom of an old fodder bin. To my bitter disappointment one was a china egg. The other I gulped down.

What in the world to do next I did not know. The only solution was to keep going if I could and to try to pass through Henton in the silence after midnight. While I was brushing myself down with wisps of straw — more with the object of keeping myself awake than of making any noticeable difference to my clothes — a car drove into the yard. It was evidently the owner of the farm coming home from his favorite pub at closing time. He put the car away in a shed, chained and locked the farm gate and entered the house.

I had a feeling that he was a confident, busy man who would have left the keys in the car, and sure enough he had. The chance was too good to be missed. In the obscurity of a car I could pass as a scruffy individual rather than a wreck. I saw myself driving straight to my London flat where I could wash, shave and change, afterwards sending an anonymous letter to the owner telling him where his property was parked and enclosing some money for compensation. It was a gift from heaven. To judge by what one read, the police seldom seemed able to trace stolen cars.

But first I had to get that gate open. The chain was padlocked tightly round the gatepost and upright. The only way of getting it off that I could see was to saw through the wood. Whatever I did had to be quick. Once the house lights were out and the TV silent, there was no hope of sawing without being heard.

One is always hypnotized by the fastening of an object and forgets the other end. I had gone off to search for tools before I remembered that gates have hinges. So I returned with a brick and a length of stout timber. With these I easily levered the gate off its hinges, and foot by foot cleared it out of the way, for my strength was not equal to dragging it aside by hand. It was the lever, too, which persuaded the car out of its shed. The slight slope of the yard did the rest.

There was no traffic in the lane and I turned into the main road at Henton feeling that my troubles were at an end. I passed sedately through Wells and then put my foot down. Fifty was all that my farmer's rattletrap would do, but she sounded in good heart and able to land me at my flat within three hours.

I think I would have got away with it if not for the cop on the motorcycle. I had forgotten him. He must have called at the farms and cottages between Henton and Westbury to ask people to keep an eye open for me and to report at once by telephone. So it may be that the farmer took a last look round when he ought to have gone straight to bed and promptly called the number which the patrolman had left. The police, for once, knew exactly what they were looking for within ten minutes of the theft without any of the usual delays in passing information through local stations.

On the outskirts of Shepton Mallet I passed a police car and in my mirror saw it stop abruptly and begin to turn. I shot into the first side road, which led me through some sort of housing estate into open country, switched out my headlights — adding crime to crime — and tried to throw off the pursuit. Luck for the moment was with me, probably because they thought they knew what my objective was, whereas I was actually twisting at random. When I was lost in a network of lanes and hamlets, I reckoned that I was safe and drove on the parking lights — not that being temporarily safe was going to solve my problem of how to reach London.

Having no map, I only knew that I was within the triangle formed by Glastonbury, Wells and Shepton Mallet. Arriving at a wild-looking lane to the west, I followed it with some vague hope of abandoning my stolen car where it would not be found quickly and of reaching Dunton's house on foot. But my lane ran down a steep little valley and came to a dead end at water with no continuation on the opposite bank. I bogged the car trying to turn, and the effort finally exhausted both mind and body. So I waded the water and climbed up a hillock beyond it, toppling over at last in a patch of woodland.

It was day again, with yellow shafts of sunlight occasionally piercing the rain clouds which blew up from the Bristol Channel. I was on top of Warminster Sleight — one of two rounded hills which I had seen too often from the road to mistake. I could see Wells and Glastonbury and the straight line of the Mendips. I could also see that a police car had joined mine down in the bottom of the steep valley. I wished to God that I had been one of the hunters looking down from my knoll upon deer drinking at the edge of the lake, instead of on too civilized meadows inhabited by nuts and policemen and children who rushed home to mother because a poor devil had a hole in his neck.

There was little I could do. Apart from my patch of cover, the slopes were bare. I dithered and my pursuers at the bottom of the valley peacefully smoked. After half an hour there was nothing whatever I could do. A van joined the car, and out hopped a police handler accompanied by a large and eager Alsatian. Ever since Fosworthy's dog which didn't exist I had been haunted by the creatures, alive and dead. More to my taste than ever was the sunlit, empty England of the hunters where there weren't any — or, if there were, their assistance was not considered worth paint and a patch of rock.

In five minutes or less — to judge by the way that damned dog was pulling on his leash — I was going to be caught in the long grind of the law. Mr. Yarrow. Well known in the district. So what the devil is he doing hiding with plenty of money and a checkbook in his pocket? Why run away? Hold him on a charge of stealing a car till he answers! Tactful inquiries might be made of Aviston-Tresco and Jedder. What they would say the Lord only knew. It might be impossible for them to stick to the bargain; or, seeing that my case was already prejudiced, they might take the risk of going straight into action.

And then I saw the only card I could play: to become what that benevolent ass who hadn't got fourpence thought I was. I ran over an inventory of my clothes. The suit I was wearing had been bought off the peg from a good, plain shop in the City which took cash and did not insist on a customer's name and address in order to pester him thereafter with sales offers. Everything else was straight commercial stuff sold in hundreds weekly by multiple stores. It would take months of a detective's time to trace my identity through my clothing; and since I was not — yet — accused of murder, it was unlikely that police would take the trouble.

All that could give away my identity were letters in my pocket and my wallet containing cards and a checkbook. I looked frantically round for a hidingplace as the cop and his dog started up the hill. There was an ash which had been split by lightning, and in the dead half a green woodpecker had been at work. The nesting hole she had started and abandoned was shallow but deep enough for my wallet and papers. On top of them I crammed in handfuls of rotten wood from the little pile at the foot of the tree. Then I ran round in a circle back to the place where I had slept, so that the dog, with luck, would not stop at the tree.

There were only seconds to spare, but at least I was now nobody at all. I had never had any dealings with the police. It was unlikely that I should meet anyone who knew me once I was safely in a cell. The only danger was the magistrate's court where, shaved and cleaned, I risked recognition.

I broke cover out onto the hillside, assuming that I ought to make the futile gesture of running away. The cops firmly and painlessly detained me and took me down to their car, where they put a few preliminary questions. Who was I? I was very sorry, but I didn't know. What had I done to my neck? I thought it was a car accident, but couldn't remember. Could I account for my movements? Well, more or less I could. I had been wandering about for some time and sleeping rough, hoping my memory would come back. I deeply regretted stealing a car, but I had been frightened and had found myself suddenly impelled to go somewhere else.

They were of course suspicious of the disappearance of any means of identification. It was obvious that I had either destroyed all papers myself or that I had been the victim of a crime. I had the impression that they were inclined to think I had attempted suicide, made a mess of the job and taken refuge in real or pretended loss of memory. The dog handler returned to the hilltop to see if his officious tyke could detect a spot where I had hidden anything. I thanked God for the woodpecker and her obliging hole at arm's length. If I had cut out a piece of turf or hidden my wallet under a stone, there might have been some triumphant tail-wagging.

I was driven down to the police station at Wells and charged with stealing a car, willful damage and a half a dozen driving offenses. When they had taken my fingerprints — which were merely going to make work for somebody — they locked me up with a cup of tea and a sandwich, and sent for the doctor.

He was just the right chap — a busy and impatient Irishman who had more respect for suffering than I deserved and a lot less for the police than they deserved. He made a very thorough examination of me and of course was interested by the recent scar on my backside. He wanted to know who had stitched it up for me. I pretended that I did not know what scar he was talking about, which may have been overdoing it. When he described it in detail, I put on a show of extreme agitation and said that I believed my wife had stabbed me. I hoped that would tie up with a domestic-trouble-attempted-suicide-lost-memory theory. At any rate it meant more complications and more time for me to play with.

When I had been supplied with a dressing gown and was lying down, trying not to show the little intelligence I had left, the station sergeant came in and asked if I was fit to be interviewed by the C.I.D.

"Almighty, man!" this admirable doctor exclaimed. "He's going straight to hospital. Can't you see that he's half starved?"

"He'd got fifteen pounds in his pocket."

"So what? Obviously from his behavior he didn't want to be found, and he couldn't go into a shop."

"Any bruise on his head?"

"No. But it isn't essential. He's had a smack on the jaw which knocked out a tooth — quite hard enough to account for concussion and lost memory, though I think all that's wrong with the boyo is that he just doesn't want to remember. Besides that, the tissues of the neck need excising and I want an X-ray of the jaw."

The sergeant asked if Detective-Constable Somebody could at least have a look at me before the ambulance arrived, to which the doctor replied that for all he cared they could take tickets at the door, but that I was to be out of there in ten minutes.

The C.I.D. man asked me a few formal questions: little more than had already been put to me in the police car. I tried to be helpful and remained deplorably vague. He was very young and out of his depth in a case of lost memory. It is possible that his senior officers were occupied elsewhere. I should have liked to listen to them taking down the bank manager's statement on Jedder's accident.

"He couldn't be this chap Fosworthy, could he," the sergeant asked, "what his housekeeper is anxious about?"

The young detective constable at least spotted my quickly suppressed interest.

"Fosworthy," he repeated. "Are you Fosworthy?"

"I don't think so," I said. "No."

The station sergeant trotted out to look up the file, and returned to say that I was not tall enough and my hair was not fair.

Because I did not know who I was, all of them treated me as a sort of non-person, speaking more openly in front of me than, I suppose, they would have done in the presence of a plain car thief. The C.I.D. man collected my coat and trousers for analysis of the bloodstains and asked to be supplied as soon as possible with my blood group. It was certainly going to deepen the mystery when they got down to putting that little lot through the test tubes. A geologist could have given them a more revealing report than a pathologist.

"They'll be jacking up the insurance premiums round here," the doctor said. "There's a farmer been carted off to Taunton General who stepped into a wooden box of .22 cartridges and they blew up under him. Would you believe it? And then look at poor Tom

Aviston-Tresco! Climbing over a gate with a pitchfork and slipping!"

"Come in threes, they do," the sergeant replied. "We had four last time, not counting motoring offenses."

"Which last time?"

"Drunk and disorderly in Gough's Cave. Turned out he was an epileptic, you remember. Next day, rape. And after two bloody hours in the C.I.D. office she comes out that she wasn't feeling like it in them clothes which was party. Same afternoon, chap leaves a suicide note in a tea caddy where you wouldn't think to look for it, and the gaffer says it's murder. Then half the night we're up on a case of breaking and entering which was just the next-door neighbor clearing the dear little sparrows' nests from the gutter which he hadn't a right to. Coincidence, that's what it is. Makes you think them bishops on the telly must have got something."

One tends in trouble to be too self-centered. It was comforting to know that I was not the most exciting and enigmatic incident in weeks and that Mysteries, as the local paper would call them, were considered routine rather than evidence of a serious crime wave.

I appreciated the sergeant's point of view. The unlikely does occur in streaks. I remember how in West Africa the shaft broke through a most improbable formation of blue clay which we were all convinced was a diamond pipe; the same evening our foreman was chased into the bush by a leopard man who turned out to be a hyena with its head stuck in an empty twelve-pound tin of bully; and two days later a mad Russian walked into camp and got a grubstake out of us with a story of panning five hundred dollars' worth of gold in two days — which we just laughed at, though it proved to be very nearly true.

I was taken to hospital, cleaned, shaved and fed. They didn't go in for psychiatry. I was cheerfully assured that when I was in a presentable physical condition I should have to appear in court and would certainly be remanded for further inquiries. Meanwhile the Taunton specialists would get back my memory for me. I was not to worry.

I did worry. I was dead certain to meet the registrar, who knew me very well after that cheerful evening together, and then Dunton would arrive as fast as his car could take him. It sounds irrational, but I dreaded that. It was one thing to tell him my story in secret and appeal to him to help me to disappear, and quite another to be forced into an uncontrollable situation in which the truth would have to come out publicly and he could hardly help at all.

A surgeon operated on my untidy neck and fussed about it, or perhaps about the jaw. I was not told. But I have never been an imaginative person where my own body was concerned — unless apologized to — and both neck and jaw felt comfortable enough to me. The stitches and dressings gave me an excuse for talking as little as possible and muttering when I did. It amused my hearty nurse that I was prepared to eat however much it hurt.

In spite of this comparative luxury, I was desperate. I could not make up my mind what to do. The old problem. Have some guts and come clean, or have some more and get clear. But I could see no hope. The hospital had my money. Some forensic laboratory had my clothes. I possessed nothing in the world but a pair of pajamas and a dressing gown — and those belonged to the county. It was enough to make a man feel he had lost his identity even if he hadn't.

The ward was a small one, with cases — chiefly accidents — which were more painful than serious. We were encouraged to move about and cheer each other up. It was hard not to be friendly, but I thought melancholy would fit my part better. I don't know if it was clinically correct; there must be cases of lost memory which would dance for joy at having lost it. However, nothing prevented me moving aimlessly about, so I used to stroll up and down the long, shiny passage outside my ward, deep in thought.

The passage ended at a T-junction, the left-hand arm of which led to the operating theater. I watched the nurses and orderlies wheeling unconscious, healthy-looking patients in, and moribund, bloodless patients out. The orderlies, often hanging about between jobs and ready to talk, accused me of showing a morbid interest. They were anxious to satisfy me that surgery was miraculous. They said I ought to think of the skill — of the craftsman, in fact, rather than of his raw material.

So that was what I did and asked questions, preserving my character of a man who disliked his unknown self and his fellow human beings as well. I wanted to know why the surgeons strolled out of the hospital beaming, whereas the patients — to the eye of a lay-man — looked only fit for the morgue. Oh, there were showers and a changing room, I was told, where the great men could freshen themselves up after the heat of the theater. They needed it. Tomorrow, for example, two of them would be at it for four or five hours.

It was quite mad, impossible to plan properly, but ly-ing awake at night I decided to risk it. After all, if I were caught, it was only one more charge to be added to the others for which the psychiatrists would have to in-vent motives — or motivations as they prefer to call them.

The operation was booked for 10:30 A.M. I hung about in and out of the lavatories until I was chased back to my ward by an angry assistant matron, but I managed to see the two surgeons come through the glass door at the end of the right-hand arm of the T-junction. One was too tall and the other running to a distinguished middle-age spread. The anesthetist, how-ever, was not far off my build and wearing a noncom-mittal dark suit.

At eleven I had to be in or on my bed for a visit by the house surgeon and an unwanted cup of tea. After that, nobody would require my presence till lunch at twelve. Bolting my tea, I mooned off down the passage and sat on a windowsill from which I could keep watch — when not staring at nothing with melancholy eyes — on at least three or four doors to the left of the T. As soon as a moment came when nobody was busily dash-ing out of wards and offices, I padded down the corridor past the double doors of the theater and jumped through the next door, which had to be that of the room I wanted. I was all prepared to burble excuses, but it was empty.

Shirts and suits were hanging neatly on a rail. Shoes and socks were scattered around more untidily. I grabbed a shirt of the right size and had just time to slide into the shower room as somebody opened the door and looked in. When it shut again, I took the anesthetist's suit and dressed in the shower room. The pockets contained only his small change. Valuables, I think, were left in individual lockers. I did not try the locks, partly because I was racing against time — never did I dress so quickly — partly because I had an old-fashioned inhibition against stealing money, whereas sheer desperation permitted me to pinch clothes.

I took off the dressing from my neck and pocketed it. The mirror assured me that most of the wound was safely under the collar and that the stitches which showed above it were hardly visible if I kept my head down. Throwing pajamas and dressing gown into a laundry basket, I covered them with an overall which was already there. Then I grabbed a fine black hat, the final touch of professional respectability, and opened the door an inch.

I could not see who was or wasn't in the corridor without sticking my head right out. The place seemed a hive of industry, healing and trolleys. I had gained a lot by talking to idle orderlies but now every one of them would recognize me, besides all the nurses who served my ward. My chances of being able to pass the T-junction and reach the glass door to the open were slim.

With growing panic I waited. It then occurred to me that some other damned doctor might want to change, and I rushed at the first comparatively peaceful moment. My own passage, when I crossed the junction, had half a dozen people in it. I passed the end in two strides holding my splendid hat in front of my face as if I were about to put it on. A door opened and shut behind me. I did not look round. Two sisters were stuck on the threshold of a ward, having a difference of opinion in low, annoyed voices; they were too occupied with each other to give me a glance. A trolley of crockery was pushed at me from a pantry, but again I had time to hide my face from the pusher. I was through the glass door and out into the car park.

I was not going to loiter there and be caught trying door handles; so I walked out of the main gate and kept walking. I looked at the cathedral clock and couldn't believe it. It was only half past eleven. I had a chance of safety if I could move quickly enough. Money did not bother me. I knew where I could get that — on condition that I was always one jump ahead of the police.

After an exasperating delay I picked up a taxi and told the driver to take me to Warminster. As we went along, I let him know that I was a Bristol surveyor and wanted to inspect a small parcel of agricultural land just outside the village. I stopped him in the middle of nowhere and then had to sneak halfway round Warminster Sleight before I could climb the knoll without being seen. By the grace of God my wallet was still in the woodpecker hole. So back again, running, to the taxi. It was ten past twelve, and the search for me in the hospital would be hotting up.

I directed my taximan to Glastonbury, but not through Wells as I wanted to see the country. It took him less than quarter of an hour. I think he wanted his lunch. It was fair to assume that the hospital orderlies would now be combing the lavatories, the basement and the gardens, and that the police would have been warned. But since nobody could know what I was wearing until the current operation was over the description of me would, with luck, be vague and might even mention that I had escaped in pajamas.

Leaving the taxi in the center of the town and telling the driver to wait for me, I dashed into a deserted alley and dealt with my smart black hat. Having served to hide my face and impress the world with my professional standing, it had now become an embarrassing property. I could not be tracked by the anesthetist's dark suit, which was just a dark suit, but that hat would give me away all over the West Country if I continued to wear it. There was nowhere I could leave it with any certainty that it would not be found, so I flattened it and stuffed it halfway down the seat of the anesthetist's trousers.

Then, hatless as I normally was, I went round a corner and into the Somerset and Dorset Bank. I kept the wounded side of my neck away from the counter and asked the clerk to tell the manager that Mr. Yarrow wanted to see him. I was shown into his office about as quickly as a stranger has ever been received in any bank, and he nervously slammed his door behind me.

"I wonder if you would be good enough to cash me a check for thirty pounds," I said.

"You really . . . ? You really . . . ?" he stammered.

Naturally he knew nothing of my adventures after leaving the barn. I should love to learn why he thought I had called on him. Blackmail, probably.

"Yes, really. Thirty in pound notes, please. After all, I am personally known to you."

I wrote out a check, and he rang for his clerk to get the money. The man came in on the wrong side of me. I kept my head well down, undoing and doing up a shoelace.

"You are still thinking of settling here?" the manager asked, compelled by his training to say something.

"No. I'm not inclined to open up at present."

I stressed the opening up. He got it, and gave a sort of pant of relief. He had evidently heard of the proposed gentlemen's agreement, but doubted it.

"About that Mr. Fosworthy's property which you recommended," I went on. "You had better know that his housekeeper has informed the police that she is worried over his absence."

"Oh, not already!"

I heard the clerk at the door and changed the position of my chair. When he was out of the room again and I had my thirty pounds I got up to go.

"If you don't mention this visit of mine, I shan't either," I said. "You may have noticed that I did not let your clerk see my neck, and I was careful to hide it when I walked in."

"I don't quite follow," he whined. "Perhaps I ought to."

"It may become clear in time. I hope it never will. But if inquiries are made, I promise you that there is no traceable connection between a man wanted by the police and Mr. Yarrow who is well known to you and was expected this morning at the bank."

"I suppose you have appropriated someone's clothes," he said with the first sign of intelligence I had ever seen in him. "I told them at the time that you couldn't go anywhere in your condition. It's not our fault. Really it was not the fault of the rest of us. I hope there is no ill feeling. You and Fosworthy — Oh God, I wish I'd never seen the place!"

"Come! Come!" I replied, shaking the limp hand which was held out to me. "Think of your spiritual development! And now you know you'll never be any good as a murderer. All gain, my dear man!"

He let me out by a side door. It was twenty to one by his office clock. The police would certainly be looking for me now in Wells, Glastonbury and every neighboring town. Still, if that poor patient — to whom I wish a long life without another hospital in it — did not go and die before the operation was over, it could not be known how I was dressed. I took out my hat, punched it into shape and paid off my taxi driver. A nearby public lavatory enabled me to put the hat back in its uncomfortable hidingplace.

I jumped on a bus which was just starting for Bridgwater. Up to then I had been intoxicated by speed and luck, concentrating always on the next five minutes.

Now that I had time to think, I realized that I would never be any good as a murderer either. Just as soon as the police started to make inquiries of taxi drivers and my man reported a customer who made a mysterious call at Warminster, they would be on my trail. I nearly jumped off the bus at the second village in a cold sweat, and had to tell myself firmly that the hell of a lot of good that would do. The taxi had driven away before I got on the bus. And, anyway, they would be looking for a man in a black hat, and I was sitting on it.

At Bridgwater I found a train leaving at once for Taunton and took it. Once clear of Taunton station, I felt more confident. After all, I was not so important that all Somerset police would be alerted in the first hour. So I went into a shop and fitted myself out with a cravat — grabbing it off the counter and instantly putting it on — together with a cheap blazer and a suitcase. I didn't care whether the police traced that purchase or not. By the time they did, I should have vanished into London.

An express to Paddington. A carefree dinner on the train. A walk to my flat as a harmless, returning holiday-maker. That was that, except that I had not got a key. However, the fire escape and the cautious breaking of the bathroom window dealt with that problem. I have always longed to know how far ahead of the pursuit I really was. I am sure the police must have guessed I took that Bridgwater bus, leaving so conveniently, but they never got on to my visit to the bank. I waited with some anxiety to be asked to confirm that I, as Mr. Yarrow, had been in Glastonbury and cashed a check for thirty pounds. However, the detective of my imagination never called.

It was, as always, from an entirely unexpected quarter that Fosworthy reentered my life. After burning the blazer and the cravat — I of course wore another one continuously — and anonymously returning the anesthetist's clothes to the hospital, I spent a peaceful week getting my breath back and trying to convince myself that justice ought to be done. I did not succeed. I think I can honestly say that it was not only the inconvenience and possible danger to myself which counted. I was also dead certain that Fosworthy would have wished me to leave matters as they were.

Disengagement, however, was shattered by a letter. Noticing the postmark, I thought it was from Gorm. It was more disturbing.

> Dear Sir,
>   I have been trying to telephone you but doesn't answer. I am a friend of Mr. & Mrs. Gorm though do not myself visit public houses who said they was sure you'd not mind my putting you a question about what I am worried about. Would like much to call on you Wednesday afternoon if convenient.
>   Yours faithfully,
>   Emmanuel Hawkins

I remembered the name as that of the farmer whose land adjoined the cart track behind The Green Man. It was he who had grown and wired the formidable hedge in which Fosworthy had been stuck. I knew he disliked fox hunting, which gave a rather tenuous connection with Fosworthy.

It was no use funking the meeting. In any case this did not smell of blackmail or of any half-baked attempt on me. *You are quite safe so long as we are,* Jedder had said. I took the simple precaution of arranging the meeting in a public place and wrote off at once asking Mr. Hawkins to tea — since he did not like public houses — at a neighboring cafe.

I felt at ease with him at once. He was an old-fashioned West Country farmer, probably the son of a farmer. Very properly he wore a bowler hat in London — a tradition much earlier than that of regular soldiers and civil servants with their rolled umbrellas and briefcases. To me, brought up with a respect for market towns, it did not seem eccentric. Indeed there was nothing extraordinary about him except that he radiated honesty and individualism. He was a contented man who could not possibly be one of Jedder's tight-lipped associates.

He let me know his business within a minute of sitting down at the table. He was that sort of character: not abrupt, but promptly weighing up the other fellow, right or wrong, and going straight to the point.

"I've come about a friend of mine," he said. "Likely as not you won't know him, but if you're going to live down our way, as Mrs. Gorm tells me you've a mind to, it won't be long before you hear tell of him. I hope so. I hope indeed he's not in any trouble."

He told me that on the morning of September 3rd he had gone down early to have a look at an ailing ewe, and his eye had been caught by a red and yellow rag in his boundary hedge which, he was sure, had not been there the day before. "If that don't belong to Barnabas," he said to himself, "I'm a Dutchman."

His introduction was detailed and gave me time to compose my face and to avoid showing any sign of recognizing the name. Fosworthy had evidently lost his handkerchief while squirming through the hedge; he always kept it in his left sleeve, and it was always of colored silk with a Paisley pattern. I don't know whether these expensive squares were his only luxury, or whether he had some theory that germs were more contented in silk.

"Hedge looked a bit worse for wear," Mr. Hawkins went on, "but he might be up to anything, Barnabas. Might have found a sheep stuck in the thorn, though there weren't no bramble and not enough fleece this time of year. And the Lord knows what he was doing of anyway.

"Well, more 'n a week later I was passing his house. When the woman as does for him comes to the door, I asks: 'Where's his reverence?' which is what we called him though he never set foot in church nor chapel. 'Hopped it unexpected,' she says. 'Trust him to leave his toothbrush or such behind him, but not every blessed thing!' Well, I asked if he was all right. He wasn't what one would call touched, Mr. Yarrow, but he had some ways which ain't yourn nor mine.

" 'I've 'ad a postcard from Reading,' she says, 'and another from London, so he's all right in the flesh, but I'm not that sure of his head. You won't believe it,' she says, 'but he's running after some 'ussy.' 'You don't say, missus!' I said. 'Yes,' says she, 'because I 'eard him

[159]

walking up and down his little library whispering *Darling! Darling!* to himself.' I told her it must have been something he read in a book. But she would have it that it was a different voice, not like him talking to the author and saying he'd got hold of the right end of the stick."

I asked Mr. Hawkins innocently if this Fosworthy hadn't made arrangements for someone to look after his stock while he was away.

"Oh, he don't farm! Always with his books and such! A vegetarian, he is. I got to know him when he was holding forth about blood sports, as he called them. Myself I ain't for 'em or against 'em. But on my land it's live and let live. If I kills a fat capon for my Sunday dinner, that's what fowls are for. And if fox kills one for his'n, that's what foxes are for."

He looked at me challengingly. In his own way he had just expressed the famous synthesis; but of course it begged far too many questions for Fosworthy ever to have noticed the resemblance.

"He's full of goodness," Mr. Hawkins went on. "That's why some folk think him not right in the head. They ain't used to it. That woman who does for him, now — blowed if she hasn't told the police that someone might shut him up by mistake!"

"You don't think that is what happened then?"

"No! What worries me, Mr. Yarrow, is that on the night he left his handkerchief in my hedge, why didn't he call and see me? So just on the chance the Gorms might have set eyes on him, I asked 'em. Old Gorm looks up his book and says that was the night you stayed in his bungalow, and if there was anything to be heard at the bottom of my land you'd have heard it. And that's why I'm here."

I said I much wished I could help him — which was true enough so far as it went.

"Well, now I've talked to you, I know you would if you could," he replied. "But what happened to the cat?"

"What cat?"

"The cat with a broken back which scratched you."

"I've no idea. It sort of struggled off," I said.

"They do hide themselves proper. I had a good look round the old stables to see if there was any trace of Barnabas. But there wasn't no cat either."

I saw the whole thing now. When Mrs. Gorm mentioned the accident and the mess in my bed, Hawkins began to wonder just whose blood it was.

"Haven't his friends any notion of where he could be?" I asked.

"A mazy lot! Chap called Jedder is the only one that's any use when he ain't shooting or hunting. And look where that's got him! And there's the vet. But I don't want to bother him with the trouble he's in himself."

I didn't take up the reference to Jedder, but I did ask what trouble the vet was in, to see what Hawkins would say about him.

"Lost his arm. Aviston-Tresco, his name is. Him and Barnabas Fosworthy was thick as thieves. But he gives me the creeps, he does. I won't have him on the place. I'm all for a man being pitiful, if you see what I mean, but not when it comes to whispering to an old cow with the staggers that he's sorry for what he has to do. Yet

I've heard folk speak of him as if he was a sort of saint. And I'll say this for him! He wouldn't hurt a fly, no more than what Barnabas Fosworthy would."

Cheerful, that was! I saw myself trying to persuade a hardheaded Somerset jury against the solid evidence of all the witnesses to character.

"*Are you seriously telling us, Yarrow, that these harmless citizens whom you attacked and maimed for life believed that murder was justifiable because there wasn't any death?*"

"*I am.*"

"*And you say they were inspired by these remarkable paintings which you yourself hoped to exploit commercially?*"

"*Well, it's not so easy as all that . . .*"

"*Answer yes or no!*"

The scene was far too vivid in imagination. When I said good-bye to Emmanuel Hawkins, I was glad that I had not given way to temptation and told him what I knew.

That mood did not last when I was alone. I asked myself what Hawkins would have done in my position. The desperate Fosworthy could easily have called on him, not me. Well, of course he wouldn't have stood for this nonsense a moment. On the other hand he would have been in the clear from the word go. Nobody could accuse him of plotting to cash in on the underground National Gallery.

I hate indecision. Time and again in my career I have lost patience with the dithering of managers and partners, and acted. That may be why I have never had steady success. I'm not a good committee man. I mention this only because I want to make it plain that I thoroughly disliked myself and could not recognize myself.

Though the horror of Fosworthy's death and my imprisonment was fading, I could no longer carry it alone. After Hawkins's visit and the suspicions which — for the time being — he had dropped, I had to ask for advice, or not so much advice as moral support. There was only one man from whom I could get it: Dunton. I called him up and asked if he would give me an hour or two of his evening. So long as I did not go through Wells and did not stop until my car was outside his front door, the chance of any policeman recognizing me was negligible.

I drove down the following afternoon. There they were again in the evening light — the mother, the daughters, the ponies, the radiance. I felt inexorably separated now from this simplicity, as if the memories which I carried into the house were visible. It was not fair, for I could not put my finger on any guilt of mine or deliberate aggression. Yet I was dirtied.

"I felt I might see you sometime soon," Dunton said as soon as he had given me a drink. He had taken me into his study, not into the garden.

I replied that if there were anything at all in telepathy, he should have felt it pretty strongly, that I spent twenty-four hours trying to reach him.

"Where's Fosworthy?" he asked.

"Why that question?"

"Remembering our last conversation. You were interested in Aviston-Tresco and Alan Jedder."

"Fosworthy is dead," I said, and told him my story.

He did not interrupt — psychiatrist's training, I suppose — until I had finished and was floundering about in morals and the climatic effect of Ynys Witrin.

"Let me have a look at the neck," he said.

I took off my cravat.

"It has not quite healed yet, but it shouldn't give any trouble. They must have intended plastic surgery later."

It struck me that he was just wasting time while he made up his mind what to say.

"You aren't afraid of me, are you?" I asked.

He gave me actual physical comfort, putting his arm round my shoulders and hugging me. He had brilliant insight. I must have needed that touch, for I nearly burst into tears.

"My dear boy," he said, though he wasn't much older than I, "I know no one more sane or less likely to commit violence."

That relaxed me, so that I could sit on the opposite side of his desk and answer as factually as I could all the questions he put to me.

"I get the impression," he said at last, "that you yourself half believe them justified."

"What? In that cruelty? And murdering Fosworthy?"

"I meant the paintings: their influence on all of you. Would I see in the mammoth and the animals what Fosworthy saw and what you see?"

I could only answer that I didn't know, that probably

he would be so interested in analyzing exactly what our associations were that he wouldn't see the thing itself. Like a painter. A painter would be too busy trying to spot how a sinuous line could carry such emotion.

He insisted that was a most intelligent remark. Yet it's obvious. Say I am looking at a rock face exposed by open-cast mining. I should be absorbed by the technical difficulties of the ore and the reasons why the company's engineer cut this way and not another. I couldn't be expected to see the beauty of the exposed strata.

"In your opinion who is responsible?" he asked.

"Miss Carlis. Entirely. But she hasn't the slightest idea of it."

I don't know what he expected me to answer. I could have said that the responsibility was mine for impulsively trying to help Fosworthy, or Fosworthy's for denouncing his creed because he couldn't find a place for love in it.

"I see. You choose outside the circle. Well, she is still decisive. At least, her evidence is. She knows it was not you who killed Fosworthy, and she will tell the truth."

"What about the influence of Miss Filk?"

"Miss Filk will break down. I know her, as you guessed. She won't stand up to ordinary police inquiries, let alone cross-examination. I don't credit all that Jedder told you. Torture is most unreliable."

I remarked that I had not got a headshrinker's couch handy.

"I'm sorry. Of course. But you're up in the light of day now with predictable human beings, not with a bunch of terrified religious maniacs in the dark. Let me explain Miss Filk for you! Leaving out technicalities, you know how brutal and cruel the maladjusted teen-age boy can be. He creates a fantastic world, through which he proves to himself his manhood. Well, she is like that. She is not in fact as markedly homosexual as she likes to think she is. So you would not be far off the truth in imagining yourself coshed by a fifteen-year-old who had seen too much violence on the telly and assumed that for real he-men it was normal."

That was significant so far as it went. If Dunton was right, I had little to fear from Miss Filk in court.

"I can't help feeling that you are still at your frontier of the imagination," he went on. "I admit the police will start with a prejudice against you, but the case cannot be as difficult as you think. I can give evidence that long ago you asked me to explain the Apology. And you have Miss Carlis and Hawkins as well."

I pointed out that Hawkins's evidence cut both ways. Aviston-Tresco would not deny that he was trying to catch Fosworthy, who was off his head and might do himself harm.

"And it's well known that he wouldn't hurt a fly!" I added bitterly.

We decided in the end that I should tactfully explore Cynthia Carlis. Indeed he offered to do it for me, but I flatly refused to have him drawn in when the consequences were unforeseeable.

What he could do and did was to call the Filk and find out what her movements were. When her number did not reply, he went to work through the grapevine of various doctors.

"She's bolted," he said at last. "Gone to America by cargo boat with a dozen Dobermans for sale. I knew she wouldn't face it. So Undine is all yours."

He insisted that her indecisive romance with Fosworthy was of great importance to her, that she appeared to have liked and trusted me and that it was common sense to go and see her. I had no great trust in common sense as a guide through the Vale of Avalon. However, she had no connection with metaphysical animism, and Dunton was sure I had nothing to lose.

I stayed the night. The atmosphere of the house was good for me and healing. Since I hoped to attain in the future such peace for myself, I shrank more than ever from giving up a year of my life to the law and newspaper publicity; but at least I found the moral courage to start safeguarding myself.

In the morning I drove to Bath and telephoned Miss Carlis. She remembered my name, but was very hesitant over accepting my invitation to lunch. Naturally she was. She knew that Fosworthy was dead and that she was in for an hour or two of explaining convincingly why she had not met him recently. But she could not refuse to see me. She suggested that I should have a drink with her at her flat before we went out. That suited me, too. From both our points of view, the preliminaries were better tackled in private than in a restaurant.

She had a charming flat and a window-boxed balcony in one of the old terraces. I wondered what eighteenth-century society would have made of her as she swept into the Pump Room; I can imagine the shady old beaux clamoring to the master of ceremonies for an introduction to such novelty. She had decided that for me she was going to be fragile and appealing. I reminded myself that if she had been some tattooed beauty of the South Seas I should certainly have been interested in the destinations and entertainment value of the patterns, and that it was ungallant to be put off merely because all that delicate latticework was natural.

I started off by saying that I had lost touch with Barnabas and that I supposed she, at least, had seen something of him.

"No."

"He never turned up at the Pavilion Hotel?"

"No."

"That's odd."

"A friend told me that he is mentally ill," she said. "Could he have been taken to hospital, do you think?"

"It seems unlikely. Hadn't your friend heard?"

"No."

So far it had hardly been possible for the poor girl to say anything else but no. Aware that she was repeating herself, she made a desperate effort to be constructive.

"Surely his housekeeper and the village know something?"

"His housekeeper has informed the police that he is missing," I said.

She could not go any paler than she was. The skin under her right ear started to throb, a pulsation made noticeable by the willow pattern. She rested her head on her hand, which suggested that the telltale sign had given her away before in moments of anger and emotion.

"Have they been to you?"

"Not yet," I assured her. "And if I am asked I shall simply say that I am as puzzled as everyone else. But I had better tell you that I know he is dead."

"How can you know? I don't see how you can know! Who told you?"

I tried to calm her down. I said I knew very well that she had nothing to do with his death and that she was only present out of kindness and affection because she had been led to believe that he had hidden himself in a cave and would not come out.

"I can't bear it! I can't bear it! It was all dark and he was killed by a thing."

"What sort of a thing?"

"A person, I suppose. A person who lived down there."

It was a close shave, but thank heaven I avoided taking the plunge and saying that the thing was me.

"How did he die?"

"He slipped."

"But the thing?"

"I don't know. It pushed him. I don't know."

She started making noises and tearing at herself. She looked as if she were going to bare her breast and beat it like some female in the Old Testament. I had not the slightest idea what to do. Probably Dunton could have carried on from that point and ended in complete command of her.

"You won't tell?" she sobbed. "Promise me you won't tell!"

"I won't. You can trust me."

She clung to me for minutes, and even put up her tremulous, prehensile lips to be kissed. It was like kissing a butterfly which had determined to flutter the conventional movements of human passion. That, I suppose, was her intention. She was ready to let me play around with the willow pattern as far as I liked in the hope of creating some intimate bond which would keep me quiet.

At the time she seemed to me as stupid as a frightened prostitute. But I do not think I was fair. After all, I had been very full of compliments on our one previous meeting, and so she naturally put me in the class of desperate admirers rather than the opposition who were unaccountably averse to her. And I must admit that there was an appealing delicacy in her approach, all the more obvious because she was trying to overcome it. I felt pity, not — or hardly not — desire. I remember thinking what a shame it was that some lover, gentle and adoring as Fosworthy, had not taken over her life at an early age. How well they could have educated each other!

Having dried her tears, I got out before they could start again, for she could not face any lunch. My principal witness had collapsed under me; and, worse still, if Aviston-Tresco and his friends were ever forced to tell her that the Thing was Mr. Yarrow, they had an independent witness of their own. The jury's taste would probably be split fifty-fifty, but the judge — if not a venerable antique — would be of just the right impressionable age to protect her from the severities of my unfortunate counsel.

I drove straight home without stopping to tell Dunton the result of his advice. Either he would reproach me for not tackling Undine with more sense and authority, or he would blame himself. I was alone again, and on the whole I thought it was better so.

Next morning I started to pack and pay my bills. I had felt worried and a coward, but fairly safe; now I felt far from safe. If that unreliable girl took an overdose of barbiturates or found her nightmares unbearable, she might spill the whole story to some comforting police matron. I proposed to be safely abroad when it happened. Fighting an extradition order at a distance would be more congenial than the relentless procession from Magistrates' Court to Assizes either as prisoner or as a witness whom everyone was trying to discredit.

The telephone rang, and I picked it up with unreasonable apprehension that the caller was going to introduce himself as speaking for the Bath C.I.D. A perfectly calm voice said:

"This is Tom Aviston-Tresco."

My good-morning must have sounded almost cordial.

"You're a bloody fool, aren't you?" he remarked as if we were old friends.

"Probably. How's your arm?"

"Stumps are never pleasant to live with. But I assure you I bear no malice."

"And I assure you that if you ever again come within my reach . . ." I began, persuading myself that I ought to feel anger, though I am not sure how deeply I really felt it.

"I am going to come within your reach," he replied. "We must talk urgently. What on earth made you stir up our little friend?"

"Would you prefer me to go to the British Museum?"

"They wouldn't believe you. They would tell you that there was no interglacial warm enough."

"Well, there was."

"It's always your assertion against everyone else's, isn't it?"

"What do you want?"

"I want you to recognize that our interests are the same. Surely you must have come across a similar position in the mining industry? Commercial greed versus the landowner's rights, and regrettable incidents on both sides?"

I retorted furiously that I had never come across anything of the sort — which was not strictly true. Yet in spite of my loathing of him it was hard not to be impressed by his outward normality. One does not and cannot know the molten interior of a man. I remember a first-class accountant who was a keen Rotarian, a masterly tennis player, and carefully emanated a conventional, suburban conviviality; but the only thing he cared for was revelation of the future by the measurements of the Great Pyramid. His wife and children were nothing but respectable cover. His only reason for excelling in his profession was to have enough money for his research — about which his socially ambitious wife kept as quiet as if he had had an Egyptian mistress round the corner. He never tried to proselytize and never discussed his religion, if it was a religion. Nor did Aviston-Tresco. His normal, useful life revolved around a central, incandescent privacy.

"We ought to talk at once," he said. "After all, we are two sensible professional men."

"If you think I am going to accept a chair or a drink from you . . ."

"That is over. I will meet you where you like and under any conditions, so long as we are alone, of course."

"Where you are?"

"In London. The West End."

I said that I would talk to him in Kensington Gardens and meet him at the Albert Gate in twenty minutes. That did not give him time for any preparations. Then I locked up my flat and gummed threads to the bottom of the door and the vulnerable window so that I could tell if anyone had visited the place in my absence.

I was a little late for the appointment. He was waiting calmly, not looking round him or showing any sign of anxiety. I hardly recognized his drawn, white face. The empty right sleeve shocked me. I wished that it had been somebody else who had made him pay a price for murder and attempted murder.

I carried two deck chairs under a tree, and pointedly seated myself on his right so that he could only reach me — if he had anything to reach me with — across his own body.

"Do you realize that we are all in considerable danger?" he asked.

[173]

"I realize that you are."

"Were. It has switched to you."

"Miss Carlis will tell the truth when it comes to the point," I said.

"She can't, because she has no clear idea what happened."

I had never quite seen it that way. When I talked to Dunton, the point I made was that she knew it wasn't me. I may have misled him.

"She must have seen Jedder charging up out of the darkness."

"I doubt if she did. He switched off his light and followed the wall. All she knows is that poor Barnabas was pushed."

"She was crying out that he slipped."

"I know. We'll come to that in a minute."

"At any rate she can't for a moment believe I did it."

"I was not there, so I have only various descriptions of the scene," he said. "Nobody saw anything clearly. What Cynthia Carlis did see seems to have terrified her to this day — a woolly thing rising from the rocks, covered with mud and blood."

"She's not so half-witted as to think it was a troll or something."

"No. But it's more comforting to believe that than what she suspects."

"What does she suspect?"

"Filk, of course!"

"But what earthly motive?"

"Jealousy."

"But Miss Filk was a little way ahead with her two

dogs," I protested. "It couldn't possibly have been her."

"Couldn't it? I have never quite understood the setup. But I see no reason why Filk should not have darted back when the lights went out. Look at it from Miss Carlis's point of view! We were all close friends of Barnabas. Only Filk had a motive. Filk's attitude to anyone who hurt her pride was that of a juvenile delinquent. Of course Miss Carlis assumed it was Filk, but rather than face it and accuse her she preferred the alternative of the unspeakable monster."

"How do you know all this?"

"Filk lost her nerve. She's gone to America. Before she left, she told her Cynthia that if anyone started asking questions about the cave she was to get in touch with me at once. She did. Last night."

"But if she thinks Miss Filk pushed Fosworthy she'll keep her mouth shut and we are safe."

I see now that the "we" committed me beyond recall — in my own mind, if not in fact.

"She would, if you had not come along — an old friend of the Fosworthy family — and claimed to know all about it. She is terrified of what you might do."

I replied that she would see sense soon enough, after I had sworn in court that Jedder cut off the light.

"Or was it you who cut it off? What help do you think you'll get from a shallow woman who is lonely and afraid? What sense as soon as she knows the monster was you? You killed one of Filk's dogs and frightened her out of her wits. You blew up Jedder and tortured him. You shot at our popular and harmless bank manager. And your subsequent disappearance was a positive epic of petty crime. Who do you think she is going to say killed Barnabas?"

"All very pretty!" I answered as coolly as I could. "But you don't want to put it to the test any more than I do. How's Jedder? Or is that another of my murders on the list?"

"They say he will recover. But I needn't tell you the police are suspicious."

He explained that Jedder's three friends — the bank manager cleared off promptly after lighting their way out and telephoning for an ambulance — had succeeded, in spite of their abject nervousness, in faking an explosion before the police arrived at dawn. They found .22 cartridges in Jedder's gun room down at the farm and put some in a flat wooden box: the sort of box a man could conceivably stamp on by accident. They bored a hole in the lid through which they inserted one of the remaining detonators and a length of fuse. Enough of the cartridges blew up to be convincing, always provided that the story of accident was never questioned. If it was, laboratory examination would prove at once that neither wood nor brass matched the splinters in Jedder's leg.

"And has it been questioned?" I asked.

"Not so far as I know. But the police are showing a tactful interest in our meetings, which they think may have been — well, bizarre in the extreme."

"What sort of bizarre?"

"Do I know? Mysterious rites. Black magic. Gunpowder and sulphur —" It was the first time I had ever heard him laugh. "They must be thinking of pantomimes and the devil popping through a trapdoor in a cloud of smoke. But if Miss Carlis starts mentioning caves — just imagine the teams of ardent potholers and the finding of Fosworthy's body! You can never make any money now, Yarrow."

I told him that I never had any such intention. He shrugged off the words as if he appreciated that I had to practice my lie. He did not try at all to believe that I had helped Fosworthy simply from pity or whatever it was. I reminded him that Fosworthy aroused affection and concern in any decent human being, and asked him how he could have treated a man he loved so cruelly. I could understand shutting him up until he promised to keep quiet about their private chapel of the animals. I could even understand that the temptation to remove me — since it was almost without risk — had been very strong. But it was beyond me, I said, that he could have brought himself to murder Fosworthy merely because he was loyal to me.

"He would have stopped at nothing to protect you."

"Then you should have faced it."

"Why? You give such strange importance to dissolution. To kill is only to deprive ourselves. A man is the same as any other higher animal. He is indestructible."

What is one to call such a creed? All the religions insist to us that we must have faith; yet what these fanatics needed was a theologian to preach to them that they must not have too much faith. In fact, now that I come to think of it, that is about what Fosworthy did. As soon as he suddenly started to value romantic love, he lost interest in his mere survival; it was what he could take with him or rediscover that became important.

It was useless to argue with a man who felt as little guilt — or as much — at putting down a human being as putting down an old cow, so I returned crudely to the problem of Cynthia Carlis and asked him what he had in mind when he telephoned me.

"I have only one arm and no strength," he replied. "But if you agree I am going to put myself in your hands."

"Like hell you are! What's the proposal?"

"I only see one way to calm Miss Carlis. I feel that Barnabas's body should be found somewhere else — on an inaccessible ledge, say, in the Cheddar Gorge where he could have fallen and remained for weeks undiscovered."

"What good does that do?"

I saw, of course, that it would be helpful if nothing more than Jedder's private, well-lit hobby were revealed whenever police investigated the cave. But removing the body did not seem to affect Undine's apprehensions one way or the other.

"The coroner's verdict is accident. Barnabas used to take long walks alone, and the medical evidence will show that he was killed by a fall," Aviston-Tresco explained. "That puts an end to her sense of the thing being unfinished and dangerous. She would even be able to send some flowers. I'm not being cynical. She is a very conventional woman and she was fond of him. Flowers would act as a tranquilizer. And what then? Filk comes rushing back from America. They settle for the unknown person in the cave — neither of us are going to name him — and live happily ever after."

I said that I certainly should not interfere and that he had better get on with it.

"Without Alan Jedder I can't. What use am I?"

"What about his three thugs? Can't you trust them?"

"One. He can stay at the hatch. The other two — nothing will ever get them near the barn again."

"I thought you people were above fear."

"Of dissolution, yes. If it were still the law, I would not mind being executed. But to be imprisoned for years, to be without my friends, the hills, the animals — that I dread. Hanging settles nothing and is humane."

"Like the vet's incinerator," I retorted in an attempt to get through his armor.

"Yes, if the animal is very small," he answered, quite undisturbed except for a note of deep melancholy in his voice.

"Or a car seat, if it isn't."

"You are a man of great courage," he said, ignoring my remark as if it were both petty and in bad taste. "Come with me and get up the body!"

"I'm damned if I do!"

"Then I must tell Cynthia Carlis that the monster was you."

"In that case it will be a long fight. I shall get a concession for the picture postcards to pay my legal expenses."

"I will accept any conditions you like. I shall be a hostage, completely at your mercy."

That was true enough so far as it went and if I could

devise absolute safeguards. So I asked him what the depth of the abyss was.

"About seventy feet. We can use Jedder's winch. If you lower me, I am capable of tying Barnabas to the rope with one hand. After you have pulled him up, you are free to pull me up or leave me there as you like."

He knew as well as I did that I shouldn't leave him there, much as I should enjoy it in principle. I told him to lay off the pathos, and asked how we were to get back through the hatch.

"You go first. I cannot stop you."

"The man up top can."

"Make your own conditions!"

It seemed to me that I ought to be able to concoct some watertight conditions. I did not entirely accept his arguments. But once Fosworthy's death had been officially accepted as accident, it became pointless to accuse me of anything. Besides that, there was a conventional streak in me which was in some sympathy with Undine. I, too, should be "tranquilized" by knowing that the body was in a West Country churchyard rather than that vile place.

"Among my other petty crimes," I said, "is the illegal possession of a .45 revolver. Any monkey business and I use it on you."

"I have to accept that."

"As soon as Fosworthy's body is in the gallery, the man on top will come down. I shall then go up the ladder and leave the rest to him."

"Provided you lend a hand from on top, if necessary."

I then saw a possible catch. There would be only one

man at the hatch when Aviston-Tresco and I went down, but there might be two or more when I was ready to come up.

"I hadn't thought of it," Aviston-Tresco replied. "I can only swear that there isn't more than one. If there was, I would use him, not you. Look at it this way! You are a far more dangerous brute than any of us. Your hypothetical other man could very well fail to kill you, as the bank manager did. You would then be justified in using that .45 of yours, closing the hatch on the bodies and going away. You are unknown. If you had been presentable and unhurt last time, you were in the clear. This time — well, I suggest a clothesbrush as well as your .45."

"What makes you think that the winch can be moved singlehanded?"

"Experience. I've done it. It just needs a crowbar to lever the wheels over ridges."

"Suppose your weight pulls it over the edge? The floor of the passage slopes towards the drop."

"Jedder used to anchor it to anything handy."

I could not remember anything handy, and warned him that the job would take some time. I then cross-questioned him about their plans after I had left and the hatch was closed up again. He told me that his associate owned land close to the edge of the Cheddar Gorge. He was going to use a tractor and trailer, the wheelmarks of which would not be new to the field. He would lower the body by a rope and then go down himself to arrange it convincingly.

"I think you ought to know a lot more about police

procedure than you do," I said. "Mysterious falls are not accepted so easily."

He talked me out of that. Anyway I did not greatly care. It was they, not I, who would have to stand the racket if they slipped up. One thing in all this was certain and constant: that they would never mention the cave if I did not.

Caution was wide awake; but, so far as his personality went, I was partly anesthetized by him as if I had been that little animal he mentioned. Apart from his obsession with the insignificance of death, he was a man out of my own West Country childhood — able, quiet, welcome in any society. And pity counted. God knows he did not deserve it! But if we limit our pity to those who do, bang goes Christian civilization.

We fixed the date for three nights later at 10 P.M. in the barn. He was too eager to discuss with me how I should travel and by what route I should reach Jedder's farm, so I told him nothing. I was not going to allow him to count on any movements of mine beyond my presence at the appointed time.

In the course of the next two days I gave much thought to the question of whether I should take my car or not and decided against it. I did not want to leave the slightest evidence of my visit to the district. There was no large public car park except in Wells or Glastonbury — where I could not risk being seen — and a car left in a small village or by the side of a lane can always arouse curiosity.

So I went down by train from London to Weston-super-Mare and then took a tourist bus to the Cheddar Caves. When the pubs opened I ate a hearty early supper, unnoticed among the crowd of sightseers, and started to walk across the bleak top of the Mendips towards Jedder's farm which was about six miles away. There was nothing on my back or in my pockets to show who I was. While I did not expect any trouble, I was taking no chances.

I was dressed in a stout windbreaker and cord trousers with a light knapsack on my back. It contained the revolver, a really powerful electric lantern and, as an insurance policy, a few cans of food and a flask of whisky. I had also the clothesbrush which Aviston-Tresco had suggested and another windbreaker, dark blue instead of dark red, which I carried partly to soften the lumps in the knapsack and partly to change my appearance in case that should be advisable. I was confident that I should be in command of any trouble underground, but the more I thought of their vague plans for the disposal of poor Fosworthy, the more I distrusted them.

I soon wished I had taken the car, for it was a foul evening with sheets of cold rain swirling up from the Bristol Channel and water gurgling into the drains of the empty road. I skirted Jedder's farm and had some trouble in identifying the right barn, which I had never seen in daylight. It was indeed on rising ground, but not easily visible, since it stood in a shallow bowl. This bowl, which I had hardly noticed as I ran away from it, was, I should guess, the result of subsidence. Beyond the end of the passage and the changing room there may at some time have been a limestone dome which collapsed.

I had three hours to wait, so I tucked myself in between a twisted thorn and a dry-stone wall alongside the track to see what I could see. The rain at last eased up. A young brood of plovers rose from the grass while the parent birds, wheeling overhead, cried what must have been encouragement to their chicks but sounded to me like thin voices of the long-dead hunters. It occurred to me that they never drew a bird, feeling perhaps that, while earthbound creatures like themselves could live again beneath the earth, it was blasphemy to immure, down there in the silence where no birds sang, the freedom of the air. Then came the gulls, one wide, purposeful arrow after another marking the high limits of the dusk. And then came a solitary car with Aviston-Tresco beside the driver.

He dropped the vet at the barn and drove away. When it was already dark, he came back with a tractor and trailer, parked them outside the barn and went in, carrying a drum of paraffin. All was silent, and I was alone with the surrounding barrows. The millennia had worn them down to a height hardly more than that of a man, but in the scrappy moonlight they doubled their true size. It was probably the effect of that hardly perceptible bowl.

I took the .45 out of my knapsack and at ten knocked on the barn door. There was dark quiet inside and I had to say who I was. They then opened up. Aviston-Tresco looked intensely relieved so far as I could judge from the hidden pools of his eyes and the stark black and white of his head in the light of the standing lamp. His companion was the man I had described to myself as the cricketer from his far too accurate missiles. I never knew his name. He had more guts than the rest, but even so tended to shy at the formidable weapon in my hand. I do not think Aviston-Tresco had warned him that the long black barrel was going to precede me wherever I went.

I thoroughly searched the pair of them, turning out all Aviston-Tresco's pockets in case he was carrying a syringe or other implement of his trade. I found nothing. He too was nameless and world-forsaken. He had only a small electric torch, a pocketknife, a few shillings, his cigarettes and matches.

The cricketer expected me to help him to remove the hay bales. I thought it best to carry on with the intimidation and remain at a range where I could not be thrown off my aim by sudden darkness or sudden movement. I reminded him that we had plenty of time and that Fosworthy had removed the bales single-handed. When he opened the hatch I told him that if at any time I found it shut, that was the end of Aviston-Tresco.

"Give me half an hour's grace," he replied. "Suppose police or one of Jedder's farmhands were trying to force the door, and I had to shut down."

I agreed to that, but warned him that he would have to get rid of his visitors in half an hour if he wished to see Aviston-Tresco alive again.

Aviston-Tresco calmly supervised the lowering of the drum of paraffin and apologized for the lack of lights down below as if I had been a casual tourist, explaining that in the absence of himself and Jedder no one had dared to start up any activity in the barn.

He ignored my menacing attitude as irrelevant. As usual this moved me to give some consideration to him.

"The rope is going to be too painful under your shoulders," I said.

"Is it?" he answered. "Yes, I suppose so. I hadn't thought."

I looked round the barn for something which would make a cradle for him and found an old cart-horse girth of canvas and leather which was still sound. If he sat on that with a light line tied round it at the level of his chest, he would have his good arm free to fend off the rock face as I lowered him.

"By the way," he asked, "where did you leave your car?"

"I came on foot. So it's no good thinking of booby traps."

He made an impatient gesture which reproached me for being unnecessarily brash. The cricketer lowered the aluminum ladder. They appeared as if about to shake hands, but did not. At any rate a current of emotion passed between them — naturally enough, I thought, when the job was to pull up their once respected prophet whom Jedder had murdered.

Aviston-Tresco went down first. He was very shaky. It gave me an excuse to get him up on my back when we returned. That would provide certain protection at the one point — emerging from the hatch — where I was still not quite convinced that I was safe.

We passed through the yellow mud of the badly shored gallery which always offended me, and down what was left of the companion ladder into the darkness. Aviston-Tresco had not seen the damage before and did not expect it. I helped him down and he politely thanked me.

In the changing room we filled and lit some lanterns, and then visited the tool store to examine the winch. Aviston-Tresco was quite right; there was nothing very heavy except the wooden stand and the main cog. A lever and ratchet raised the stand on its wheels, which were a good foot in diameter, or lowered it to rest firmly on the ground.

I measured and tested the rope, which was first-class stuff. Jedder was no builder, but reliable in the mechanical tasks of a seaman. It was obviously impossible to keep Aviston-Tresco covered during all this preparation, so I made him sit down at a distance and shone my torch on him from time to time to see that he was behaving. When I had fixed the sling, I told him to walk slowly ahead of me holding a lantern while I trundled the trolley along behind with another lantern and some tools lashed to the winch. I was glad of the activity, for the passage began to oppress me as soon as we were engaged in it. A pigsty smell hung in the still air, undoubtedly left by me. The ghost of one's own animal stench is an odd and disturbing thing to revisit.

Aviston-Tresco stopped at my alcove and looked at the ashes of the fire and the bones and scrapings of my revolting diet.

"The working floor," he murmured.

We passed through the great cave by following the wall and the useless wires of the lighting system. Even with our two paraffin lamps and my electric lantern, that was the only sure way. At this point I had an attack of shivering. Poor monster! He had only been desperate and frightened. He was still unduly nervous and would have shot at the first sound from nothingness.

I had never looked down the precipice on the left of the wired passage, having no interest in it before Fosworthy's death and only paraffin lamps afterwards. Without lying on one's stomach on the sloping, slippery track — which I had no intention of doing — it was hard to see anything but the irregular wall of the cave on the far side.

Keeping Aviston-Tresco well away, I explored the edge of the drop. Farther along the passage, the lip curved out a little, forming a promontory which ended in a lump of rock. It gave an illusion of safety while kneeling alongside, for there was enough of it to lean against. I screwed up the lens of my fine new light and threw a beam on the bottom of the cleft, more like eighty than seventy feet below. It was wider than the top, and dry. Boulders and rocks covered the floor, none of them water-worn. Plainly a cave roof had at some time fallen in. Among the smaller rocks was a long, narrow one with a white patch at the far end of it. It was Fosworthy's body.

I now knew where to site the winch so that Aviston-Tresco would come down more or less in the right place. Its lack of stability bothered me; as an engineer I probably tended to fuss too much. In the end I squared off a crack in the cave wall at ground level, and pushed into it the back of the stand, supporting the front on chocks. My companion watched all this disinterestedly.

I made him sit in the girth and ran a line round the canvas and his chest, telling him to hang onto the rope with his good arm. Owing to the overhang he would not have to fend off the rock face, but he would probably spin. I promised him that there was no risk of the rope fraying since I had chosen a channel for it which was smooth with a film of deposit. He submitted resignedly to every one of my suggestions.

He wriggled over the edge, and I let him down slowly. The winch was so close to the cave wall that I had to work it with my back to the drop, shouting to him at intervals for a progress report. He said that he was spinning, yes, but not fast, that he was well out from the rock and could not bump into anything. He told me when he was near the bottom, and I let out rope gently until the weight came off it. Then I went out to my promontory to help him with a beam of light. He himself had only his pocket torch.

He had landed right by Fosworthy's feet. So far as I could see, he was not at all shaken by the proximity. He slipped out of his lashing, and then to my alarm cast off the sling from the rope. I shouted to him to leave it alone since with only one hand he might not be able to attach it again by a secure knot, but he paid no attention. He tied the rope tight round Fosworthy's waist and told me to go ahead. I wound the drooping bundle up as respectfully as I could, reminding myself that affection, even as casual as mine for Fosworthy, should not be disturbed by the results of decomposition.

When I had stretched the body out at some little distance, I lowered the rope again and returned to the promontory in order to direct Aviston-Tresco how to attach the sling if he was inclined to do it carelessly. He was sitting on a boulder smoking a cigarette and making no move towards the dangling rope.

"Are you tired?" I asked.

He did not raise his voice. It came faintly echoing up in a clear, articulate whisper as if he were speaking from the darkness alongside me instead of eighty feet below.

"No," he replied, fiddling with his shoelace, "not very. But I am not coming up."

"Why not?"

"Because this is the end for me."

I tried to encourage him. I thought he had merely given up, or perhaps had at last been overcome by guilt in the presence of what was left of Fosworthy. I was eloquent about his hills and animals.

"You don't understand, my dear Yarrow," he said. "There is nothing in this life to detain a man who loves his profession and can no longer follow it. I have left a note in my surgery that I intend to walk out into the mud of the Parrett until it has me. It will be hopeless to search for my body once the tide has come up and ebbed again. But I shall not hang about down here to embarrass you."

He took off his shoe which of course I had never thought of searching. I could hardly see what he held between finger and thumb. At the end of the beam was just a tiny spark of reflecting glass.

"But I can never get you up," I reminded him. "Think, for God's sake, of Cynthia Carlis! Suppose she does tell what she knows and the place is full of police. It's no good hauling up Fosworthy and leaving you."

"Miss Carlis will never talk, Yarrow. She believes Filk did it, and that is that. My explanation to you was deliberately a little complex."

"But then why bother with all this? Why not jump?"

"It was essential, you see, to keep you happily occupied. I have noticed that you are always entirely absorbed by any mechanical task."

Again I asked why.

"You might have kept an eye on the hatch. You might have decided that there was no reason why our friend up there should not be with us. I was afraid you would."

"Where is he?" I shouted.

"Gone home with his tractor and trailer. He knew what I intended."

Gone home! How could I guess? All my plans and precautions had been founded on the natural assumption that Aviston-Tresco wanted to get out alive. I took man's normal fear of death for granted in spite of so much evidence that this particular man had none.

"I hope that you will soon forgive me," he said. "It will all seem so unimportant when you and I and Barnabas meet."

The cave wall transmitted every sound. I swear that I actually heard the crunch as he put the capsule between his teeth. It took effect at once.

I did not yet go back to the hatch to see if he was telling the truth. I knew it. I realized that the draft in the passage had long since stopped. It was barely noticeable, a mere caress of ice on the cheek, but always there when the hatch was open.

I went and sat on the winch, bewildered that he would sacrifice his life to insure my eternal silence, bewildered by his absolute, proved certainty of survival. What a creed for soldiers! Well, but there is nothing new under the sun. The fanatics of the early armies of Islam believed in it and were unconquerable.

The thought passed through my mind that I might as well slide over the edge myself. But while I was considering this in all honesty, I put out one of the lamps. There was no avoiding the irony of that. Something in me wanted so badly to live that it was already economizing paraffin. I must be the very opposite of Aviston-Tresco — a creature of simplicity, never seriously questioning instinct, never doubting that, whatever the purposes of life are, one of them is to live it.

It was no good sitting there. First, I rushed to the hatch in a wild access of optimism. Perhaps Aviston-Tresco had not in fact told the cricketer of his intention. But he had, and it was shut. Then I wallowed in many minutes of emotional despair. There would never be any opening of the cave by those spiritless, guilty cowards up above on the Mendips. Jedder might do it if he could limp his way down, but that day was far off. The Gate of the Underworld had closed on me as inexorably as on my only companions.

In order to generate in myself some sense of calmer acceptance, I decided to revisit them. In the Painted Cave I used, as always, only lanterns; they were still far brighter than the blubber lamp and its eddying pencil of smoke, on which the artist had counted to give the stir of movements to his hunters while they killed and were forgiven. There they were, as they had been for the last twenty-five thousand years, abandoning themselves to their environment with a gaiety which we have forgotten. The interrelationship between them, the deer, the horses and the accepting mammoth belonged to the science of ecology rather than anthropology.

Was it this to which Aviston-Tresco looked forward? Well, no. I cannot believe that he primitively wanted happy hunting grounds. Then what parallel, in his own terms, did he foresee? Some sort of unity with all other animals, I suppose, within which his own individuality could be expressed. I can go a bit of the way with him. We are all uneasily aware that man is on his way to the ant-heap community, and that he knew more of the true business of living when he was old and diseased at forty. We are too fascinated by the actual time we remain alive. Their life of forty years held just as much in it as ours of eighty, just as a year at ten is twice the length of a year at twenty.

"What the hell shall I do now?" I silently asked them. "Here I am with enough food to keep me fit for two or three days and allow me to work for a week longer. What would you have done with only your horn and bone and flints and bits of wood? You obviously thought of life and death as a kind of continuity, but I take it you didn't give up until some other carnivore was asking you for forgiveness."

Their answer was not very satisfactory. They were no more mystical than boy scouts. They suggested that I had steel tools and the knowledge to use them: in fact that I was about on a technical level with Arthur.

Arthur. His name incongruously came into my head because I was staring at him. Subliminal advertising.

At the back of a recess to the left of the overhang I made out a scratched engraving of four women — the exaggerated spearheads of their breasts establishing sex — sitting upon a line broken by the conventional curves of water. No doubt about that. One cannot mistake that the deer of Lascaux are swimming. With the women was one recumbent man, dead or sleeping, wearing the head of a horse. Who was he and why was he being ferried in canoe or dugout across the Lake of Avalon? Can a folk memory from the Paleolithic still exist as a fairy story?

An important discovery? My mind, stunned and taking refuge in the only companionship there was, thought so at the time. Now I doubt it. One might as well say the man with the horse head was the origin of the chess knight, which is manifest nonsense. No, I had merely joined the club of Glastonbury eccentrics. I have probably been nearer to them, all along, than I ever suspected.

But the Arthur/steel association stuck. Though nothing except explosives or millions of years of flowing water was going to be much good against the limestone of the Mendips, there must be other objectives if I applied a bit more imagination to the search for them.

When Fosworthy and I had been alone, we accepted the impossibility of either reaching or lifting the hatch and tried to find another way out. Afterwards, when I was alone, the right game was to keep hysteria under control and wait for the hatch to be opened. But now, at last, led on by my little friends — who reminded me that tools are tools — I saw that my best bet was to tackle the work of man. I had not been at all successful in tackling the work of nature, whether it was rock or the human minds of Undine and Aviston-Tresco.

I turned away from the hunters by the once warm waters of Avalon and set off to the hatch with all the lights I could collect. If Jedder had bedded the brick frame of the hatch into surrounding rock, I was done; if he hadn't, there was a hope. But it was hard to find out what method of construction he had in fact used, since there was no ladder from which to inspect it. What was left of the companion ladder was firmly cemented in place and useless anyway. Only the outer handrail was intact.

The shaft was smoothly lined with brick. Fosworthy and I had already found that it was impossible to climb to the top by piling up bits and pieces, and I was now clean out of wood in useful lengths, having sawed it all up for my fire. As a last resort I could knock out the shores and props from the gallery, but I did not much care for that. The roof, as it was, had a tendency to spew bits of itself out.

I went back to the winch to fetch the pick and cold

chisels. Then I started to test Jedder's mortar. No trouble there! He had been using as much material as possible from the cave itself, and his sand was full of clay. Even so, it was a long, tedious job to knock out the bottom course of bricks, especially since I needed them and did not wish to break more than I had to.

By five in the morning — if there had been any morning — I had removed six courses and piled the unbroken bricks at the entrance to the gallery. By then my back was aching and hands beginning to blister, so I knocked off and ate a can of bully and a raw onion. I was thankful that I had packed a small store of food, though expecting to use it in the open, if at all. At the bottom of my knapsack was the clothesbrush. How ingenious Aviston-Tresco had been! The suggestion of the clothesbrush, which he knew I was never going to need, was a wonderful confidence trick.

I forced myself to rest, awake or not, for six hours. Sleep was less easy than during my first imprisonment. Then I wanted to get away from pain and terror; now, I was only suffering from an unaccustomed form of exercise. I was also conscious of the stench — partly of blood, partly of my rank former self — which my bed of sheepskins gave out when they were warmed up by my body. It reminded me that in envying the freedom of the hunters I was inclined to forget their living conditions. But we are fussy. It is said that we should be revolted by the stinking of even the eighteenth century.

When I resumed my task, it was much easier. I could now swing a pick at the level of my knees, get the point behind the bricks and often detach several at a time. As soon as I was working above the height of my head, I built a platform of sound bricks to stand on. Shifting the platform round the shaft began to take more time than the actual demolition, but that went fast — sometimes too fast at points where Jedder had not properly bonded his brickwork into the rubble of the shaft. When the whistle blew for supper, I was working twelve feet from the ground with eight or nine more to go.

Twenty-four hours had passed since I entered the cave with Aviston-Tresco. I was cautiously pleased with my progress, though aware that the next shifts were going to be far more complicated and dangerous. I had to make a sort of steep staircase out of the loose bricks; since there were not enough, the structure was too narrow and horribly unstable. Swinging a pick was impossible. Even using a hammer and cold chisel was alarming. I never felt secure on my teetering staircase unless I had one hand on the wall of the shaft. An uncontrollable fall in a shower of bricks was a nasty prospect when I could not afford a sprain, let alone a fracture.

However, I could now examine the underside of the hatch. Its frame was not let into rock or concrete; it simply stood on the top course of bricks. Under that were left some twelve more courses, completely unsupported. With all the weight of hay on top of the hatch, the brickwork might at any time come down with a wallop, dropping the hatch on me while I was chipping away underneath. I was none too happy, either, about the exposed rubble through which the shaft had been dug. There was a sizable trickle of water in one place, and in another, threatening little showers of pebbles and earth.

Some sort of scaffolding was essential, allowing me to get both hands to the job and checking the falling hatch while I jumped for my life. But I could not see what to use nor how to support it. So I opened up my last can of food, took a generous shot of whisky to help imagination and slept on the problem.

The solution was fairly clear in the morning — which turned out to be midday by my watch. Working down from the top, I changed my staircase into a pillar. Opposite, I built another pillar as high as I could reach. I sawed off the handrail of the companion ladder and cut it to fit the diameter of the shaft. My difficulty then was to build up the second pillar to the height of the first and hoist the beam up to rest on the pair of them. I felt hopeful that the pillars would hold once my weight was on the cross beam.

Meanwhile, hold they would not. When the top of the second pillar was beyond my reach, I carried on building by balancing single bricks on the end of a last piece of two-by-four timber, holding it up like a caber-tosser and sliding them into position. Twice the whole stack fell down. And when at last I had finished it I could not get my beam up.

The only possible method was to hoist it up by means of a hook driven into the wood of the hatch, but there was nothing at all in Jedder's stores which would serve or could be bent to serve; nor had he got a drill. I cursed blind and sat on my knapsack, in which nothing remained except the damned clothesbrush, some biscuits and the revolver. But that was it! There was my hook and there was my drill.

I dismantled the two pillars and turned them back into a stair. I fired a shot obliquely into the wood of the hatch, and hammered and twisted the barrel into the splintered hole until it was firmly jammed. The butt, turned upwards, then formed a neat and reliable hook. It was the only use I had ever found in all my life for that large, clumsy weapon.

When I had hung a length of rope on it, I changed the stair into two pillars again. That sounds simple; but it took six blasted hours of trial and error and repeated rebuilding before I had hoisted the handrail of the companion squarely into position on the bricks. I had just enough energy left to climb up the rope and sit on the beam, not caring greatly whether the whole crazy structure collapsed or not.

By this time I felt that I would rather be squashed than climb down again, probably bringing a pillar with me. So I knocked out the last courses with hammer and chisel, leaving the frame supported on only eight bricks. Three of them stayed where they were by the magic of inanimate bodies. Five on the other side were cemented — pretty well for Jedder — to a solid paving stone on the floor of the barn.

It looked as if I might now have a future provided that I got out from under quick. I slid down — half a pillar and the beam came down as well — and removed knapsack and tools into the comparative safety of the gallery. My watch surprised me. It was already afternoon in the outside world. As I thought it unwise to attempt the breakout when there might be people within earshot, I ate my biscuits and rested.

I could only doze uneasily, while obsessed by all the incalculable ways in which hatch, shaft and barn floor could collapse, as well as by the awkward evidence I was leaving behind; bloodstains, fingerprints, mess and a couple of bodies. I was sure that Aviston-Tresco had told the truth and really left a suicide note, since his whole objective was to end once and for all the sequence of events which had started with his imprisonment of Fosworthy. When his body was found, analysis would show he had poisoned himself. But why hadn't he drowned himself in the Parrett as he said he was going to? And who lowered him, alive or dead, down that hole?

Well, the question marks had to be left, but I could ensure that there would never be easy answers. I suddenly realized that with a bit of luck I could close the entrance so convincingly that no trace of it would remain. If at some future date an unknown potholer found his way into the cave by a new route, he could work out the tragedy for himself. Digging to see where the wires led beyond the companion ladder, he would come upon Fosworthy's body. Then, or perhaps earlier, what remained of Aviston-Tresco would be discovered. Coroner and police could spend months trying to work that mystery out. Nothing fitted, but there was no suggestion of murder, no third person concerned. Fosworthy had apparently been overwhelmed by a landslide as he tried to get help.

So I left the winch where it was with the rope hanging down and I carried Fosworthy's body into the gallery. I knew that he would have forgiven this. He was always so anxious to protect me. "A mere envelope," he would have said. "If you consider, my dear Yarrow, that it may relieve you from the grave embarrassments for which I was inadvertently responsible, it is entirely at your disposal."

The next task was admittedly chancy; but every stress and strain of that gallery was familiar to me and I knew what I was doing. I began to knock out the props, starting from the top of the companion. The result was instant and spectacular. Access to the cave was already closed. Working backwards towards the shaft, I slammed out some more of the shoring over Fosworthy's body. When I had prized loose a boulder in the roof, I jumped back to wait for the crash.

It worked. The gallery had ceased to exist except for some twelve feet at the entrance to the shaft, and Fosworthy's body was buried. But while the dust was settling and I was shining my torch on the yellow wall which faced me, there was a roar like the end of the world behind.

At first I thought that I, too, was buried. My feet were knocked from under me and I felt drowned in dust and debris. But when my torch could show anything, it showed that the joists above me were still intact. What had happened was that the waves of my minor earthquake had brought down the hatch, with the hay and half the shaft as well.

I was caught in my bit of crumbling tunnel. I ac-

cepted dully that it might be anything from five minutes to a day or two days before I could dig myself out.
By God, that vile hellhole had trained me in patience!

Clearance of the entrance with pick and hands was
very slow, since bricks, debris and hay bales had to be
stacked in the gallery. Calculation on the back of an
envelope showed that there must be more solid matter
in the shaft than would fit into my twelve feet of space.
However, I did at last arrive at a sort of working face,
though there was very little room to work at it.

The whole mass settled as I drove my sap into the
bottom and I could now see that it was composed of
solid cubes — the bales — with loose rubble and brick
between them. This pattern allowed some air to come
through. I had been wondering for some hours why I
was not gasping for breath. Jedder's binder twine must
have been exceptional stuff or else he specially tied
these bales to resist frequent lifting. Few of them had
split open.

I found it just possible to rearrange them in the shaft
itself so that I could burrow upwards from one to another. Showered with rubble and now half asphyxiated,
I twisted and turned and shoved through the darkness,
feeling like an earthworm trapped under a haystack. It
was impossible to take with me lanterns, knapsack or
anything. At last I saw a crack of light between bales
and pushed until my shoulders were through. As soon
as I could free feet and legs from the various unseen
bulks and weights which held them, I was out.

But the safety of night had gone. It was eight o'clock

and there could be possible visitors to the barn unless the cricketer had locked the door and taken away the key. A shaft of early sunlight slanting through the glass panes in the roof and lighting up the golds of old wood and chaff cheered me as much as the food and drink for which I longed. Everything was silent, but somehow too breathless, too close to the absolute silence underground. I remained still, listening, in the shelter of what was left of the stack of bales. How can one recognize the stillness after sound when one has not actually heard the sound? Then someone unmistakably approached the door and rattled it.

"If it were locked the first time, likely it be locked the second," said a dry Somerset voice.

Another, more standard-English voice replied that there was nothing to be gained, either, by looking through the window a second time.

"Aye, but I'll just 'ave another peep for luck."

What window? Well, it had to be in the room to which Jedder and Aviston-Tresco had retired to consider our fate when Fosworthy and I were tied up and helpless on the floor. I tiptoed across the barn and opened the door. There was a very dirty window, with a pane broken, screened by a piece of heavy chain-link fencing. I quickly shut the door and lay down beneath the window sill.

The two came round the barn and peered through. There was nothing much to see — an old roll-top desk and chair, and some shelves stuffed full of files and back numbers of farming magazines. I guessed at once that the room was a fake, rigged up so that Jedder could always have the excuse of paperwork for shutting himself up.

"Private office, like," the Somerset voice announced.

Its owner was probably a stockman on the estate. The other fellow sounded like a bailiff new to the place and taking over while Jedder was in hospital.

"Two sets of books, I wouldn't be surprised," he said.

"Or 'ymnbooks and such."

"Hymnbooks?"

"Used it as a chapel, some of 'em did. I seed 'em take some birds up 'ere once."

"Did you now? I wouldn't have thought Mr. Jedder was one for a bit of slap and tickle in the hay. Well, we'd better be getting along. You can see there's no one there."

"Didn't say as there was, did I?" replied the Somerset voice. "What I said was that I 'ears a kind of big whoosh when I were walking 'ome last night. You wouldn't 'ave thanked me for bustin' in on your beauty sleep, but daylight's daylight."

It was also clear that both of them had heard some muffled noise while I was breaking out, and had been intently listening as I had.

"Nothing wrong with the barn, is there? What you might call *wrong*?"

"Not that I knows of. Not like Marty's."

They talked for a bit of Marty's, which seemed to be a deserted cottage troubled by a poltergeist or similar nuisance. I could understand the underlying train of

thought. Meetings. Spiritualism. And then the appearance of this mysterious, dusty little room as seen
through wire and a broken window.

"What was he doing when he was blown up?" the
bailiff asked.

"Know what I thinks? Changing the shot in 'is cartridges!"

"But they say it was a box of .22."

"They can say what they've a mind to. What I says is
that he was emptying out No. 5 shot and filling of 'em
up with No. 7."

This astonishing theory puzzled both me and the
bailiff.

"But what for, when he could go out and buy sevens
if he wanted them?"

"Because 'e didn't like for it to be known, of course!
What would you say yourself to a man what uses No. 7
for partridge and hare? Unsporting, you'd say! Won't
kill 'em clean, you'd say!"

"Well, I'll buy it," the bailiff replied. "Why wouldn't
Mr. Jedder want to kill clean?"

"Because he liked to look at 'em tender-like when
they was floppin' about and then wring their little
neckses. Watched 'im at it time and again I 'ave when I
been out with the guns!"

An ingenious theory, and built out of accurate observation! I remember asking Dunton if one heard something like *Bang, bang! Sorry, sorry!* Well, I wasn't so far
out. I do not for a moment suppose that Jedder avoided
killing clean — a most difficult thing to do, anyway —

but when he had winged a bird or lamed a hare, he evidently did pick it up "tender-like" and silently gave it the Apology.

What was of real importance was this talk of monkeying in some way with cartridges, not accidentally stepping on them. If that was local gossip, it must have been considered by the police. From their point of view, inflammatory substances could still be lying about. I was tempted. It was a risky game to reduce the barn to a charred heap of undefinable rubble in broad daylight, but I reckoned that I had nothing to lose and a more tranquil future to gain.

The pair outside the window decided that it was none of their business to break into the barn, but that the police had better be informed of the mysterious whoosh. As soon as they were safely out of sight, I began with the tractor, which I knew must be in working order in spite of its dilapidated appearance, since Jedder used it to drive his dynamo. It took me five precious minutes to start. I became very uneasy lest I might be compromising my escape by an impulsive piece of foolishness.

At last it fired, and I drove it into the corner of the barn above the gallery. I was sure that its weight would prove to be the last straw for the last twelve feet of tottering shores. It was. The tractor sank into a yard-deep hollow, and the wall above it was instantly zigzagged by a promising crack in the stonework. By the time that the tractor and the subsidence had been covered by a shower of roof tiles and charred beams, nobody but a

fire assessor was likely to be curious about the difference of levels or even to notice it. And it was absolutely
certain that Jedder would never put in a claim to his
insurers.

In fact he could never take any action at all. He could
not risk replacing the barn and allowing builders to explore the foundations. He could not reopen shaft and
gallery without a lock-up building to hide his private
excavations. I felt conscience-stricken at the main loss,
the only important loss, and consoled myself by the
thought that if the paintings had remained undiscovered for a thousand generations, they could well spend
one more in the darkness. I suspect now that this consolation was too easy. Jealousy entered in — the same
jealousy which was the simplest of all the motives of
Jedder, Aviston-Tresco and their friends. I resented
those lolly-sucking tourists who would file hour after
hour past a beauty which should only be observed in
silence and long contemplation.

I piled bales and hurdles against the tinder-dry wood
of the old cow stalls, put a match to the bonfire and to
what remained of the hay as well. Then I dashed into
Jedder's fake office, shutting the door against the in-
ferno in the rest of the barn, ripped out the screen over
the window, hurled shelves and papers to the floor, lit
them and cleared out.

But I had left it too long, thanks to the obstinacy of
that damned tractor. As I dropped to the ground, I saw
a car turn into the track from the main road. It was all
of three hundred yards away, and I hoped that the

smoke beginning to billow from the window had ob-
scured my outline. Edging along the wall until I had the
building between myself and the car, I ran for it.

Almost at once I had to break into a casual walk. As
my head came over the skyline of the little depression, I
saw two chaps — presumably those whose conversation
I had overheard — hurrying up the hill from Jedder's
farm. There was no cover of any sort, not even a dry-
stone wall for a quarter of a mile, so I played the con-
scientious taker of exercise and stepped out. They paid
no attention to me until they were high enough to see
the disaster. Then they let loose at me with shouts
which I could hear above the crackling of the flames. I
walked on, making my guilt certain. Anyone who
showed no curiosity at the sight of a fire was plainly
worth detaining.

A quick glance over my shoulder revealed the appal-
ling fact that the car was a police car. Two peaked caps
which had been helplessly watching the blaze bobbed
back into the front seat. The car immediately returned
up the track in order to patrol the main road and prevent me crossing it, while Jedder's two employees began
to pound after me over the downland. It was small
comfort that I no longer faced a charge of murder. Ar-
son would do nicely, forming a climax to all the crimes
of the unknown when he was delivered to Wells police
station.

My only chance was a belt of trees on the near hori-
zon. Though my legs were too weary to run far uphill, I
reached it a minute ahead of my pursuers. One end of
the belt started from the road; the other ran towards

more broken country with a few small coppices. Any hunted creature would have gone hard and straight for the cover, so I chose not to. Or it may have been that I refused to run any more.

I turned towards the road and dropped into a hollow hardly large enough to hold my body. Jedder's two men took the obvious line and raced down the trees, one on each side of the belt. That allowed me a rest, but there was no chance of crossing the road and breaking away to the northeast. The police car was within twenty yards of me and remained there. I could imagine what its aerial was saying.

It was now only a quarter past nine. The sun had gone, and low, black clouds drove across the moorland bringing sheets of bitter rain. I crawled off through the trees until it was safe to rise to my feet and take stock of my very nasty position. I could strike straight down the open escarpment into Westbury, but there was pretty sure to be something waiting for me by the time I hit the Cheddar road. Alternatively, I could work my way east through such cover as there was, but that would lead me far too close to the village of Priddy and its network of busy lanes. I was not torn and bleeding this time, but inevitably I looked at close quarters as if I had been buried alive, as indeed I had been. The only sound move seemed to be to lie up till nightfall on the top. It was open as a chessboard, but at least the squares had stone walls round them.

Looking back, I am sure that I ought to have taken advantage of the fact that contact with me was broken and to have slunk away quickly in any direction under cover of the walls; but I did not foresee that interest in me would be so intense. Lunatics who set fire to lonely barns and ricks are a pest and cannot be left at large. And the police, of course, being suspicious that there was more to it than that, wanted badly to talk to me. There was the doubt as to what had really happened to Jedder; there was the disappearance of Fosworthy; and there must have been a big question mark over the unknown fire-bug since his build corresponded to that of the car thief who had escaped from hospital.

I settled for a shallow pit where elder bushes gave a little shelter from the direct lash of the rain. About three in the afternoon I had to get out of there smartly. Four men — two of them the fellows who had chased me — were advancing well spread out across the moorland as if they knew the square mile in which I must be. It was certain that they would search such an inviting patch of cover. I was safer in the misery of the open.

I got away from my pit unseen, moved north across their front and found the road empty of traffic. The police car was still there, but round a corner watching the straight ribbon of wet tarmac which fenced me in. I nipped across and was seen by a motorcycle cop concealed in a gateway only two hundred yards away. He spent a few seconds reporting my presence through his walkie-talkie, taking his eyes off the road and its verges. I accepted the crazy chance offered by his very proper devotion to routine, recrossed the road and hurled myself back into the ditch I had started from. The patrol car was on the spot almost at once, and the whole lot of them except the driver charged off on my supposed track. I never saw them again. For all I know they may have reached the low ground to the northeast before they were whipped in and returned to kennels.

With the police out of the way, I took to the open fields again but was sighted by one of the party of locals while jumping a gate. I tried to break back. It was no use. So I ran crouching under the cover of a wall, again at a right angle to the course of the party. The blasted elephant-gray world did not affect visibility. Morale finished, I cursed myself for ever thinking of settling in such country. Arthur, holy Glastonbury and its lunatic fringe were welcome to this half-world through which I scuttered from wall to wall like a bedraggled and exhausted hare.

I threw off the pursuit among the barrows, wishing to God that one of them would open, as our ancestors dreaded, and that the grinning Inhabitant would beckon me in. His stone home could not be much worse than where I had been. At last I found myself within fifty yards of the barn. It was a black shell, not even steaming in the rain. The wall against which the hay bales were stacked had fallen outwards. The depression was hardly noticeable, being partly filled with charred beams and shattered tiles among which was the gaunt, twisted frame of the tractor.

The police and the curious — if there had been any — had gone. The place stood derelict in the pouring rain as if it had been burned down years ago instead of that very morning. I cannot analyze what put it into my head to take refuge there. Shelter? There was none. Familiarity? Perhaps, in the sense that a ghost might be so lonely that it wished to return to hell. Warmth? That, I am sure, counted. A wave of warmth came from the site of Jedder's office.

Yet it was the blocked shaft which attracted me. The surface of fine ash from the hay was soapy as scum on a pond, but underneath it was black, dry and powdery. The deposit looked as if it were evenly spread, but I knew that it could not be. The bales at the top of the shaft, between which I had pushed my way out, must also have caught fire, leaving a hollow. I burrowed into it backwards, smoothing the disturbance of the surface as I went. My head ended up in the shadow of one of the tractor wheels; it could not, I hoped, be recognized as part of a human being, since it was black as the surrounding ash and camouflaged by fallen tiles. It was still very hot under the tractor, but my clothes were too soaked to be singed. I had to be careful not to expose bare skin or to touch anything solid.

In a few minutes two of my pursuers were also at the ruins. They searched perfunctorily among the fallen beams at the other side of the barn where the blackened wall still stood. That was the only spot which was not wide open for inspection. After one of them had burned his nose in the shadows, they decided it was far too hot for a hidingplace.

They sloped off up the track, all enthusiasm for the hunt gone, shoulders huddled under the lash of the rain. I stayed where I was, deliciously warm and waiting for darkness. I may even have dozed off, for I suddenly found my nose full of ash and had a fit of sneezing. There was nobody to hear. Except for the incessant patter of the rain, my resting place was as silent as Fosworthy's.

In the west a strip of the leaden sky melted into a band of sickly yellow, the only sign that there ever had been and would be again a sun. I lay still while the twilight deepened. I was incapable of making any plans. My only comfort was that hands, face and clothes were black, and that I had become as nearly an invisible man as any fugitive could wish for.

I heard a car drive down the track in the last of the dusk. The occupant got out and quietly closed the door. From my position I could not see who it was, but I guessed by his stillness that we had met and that, hearing of the fire, he was paying a last, lonely visit either to mourn the dissolution of Aviston-Tresco or of the shrine where he had once found a spiritual security. He came round the ruins until he was looking straight at me across a tumble of fallen stones.

The chance was too good to miss. I stirred in my bed of ashes trying to get a sound foothold and at the same time to avoid touching the hot steel of the tractor. My clumsy struggles infuriated me when I wanted to leap straight for his throat before he could beat me to the car. But he did not wait. He gave one queer, choking cry and ran. I could not make it out at all until I myself was clear of the ashes and racing for the abandoned car. What he had seen was the closed shaft bubbling and seething as a black, blind, incinerated thing struggled to get out. Which of the supposedly dead he thought it was I do not know. His overwhelming sense of guilt must have aided the nightmare as well as more solid memories of my own monstrous refusal to die.

On the lip of the hollow he regained control of himself and turned to look back. It was too late. I was already sitting in his car. Ten minutes of frantic driving brought me over the northern slopes of the narrow Mendips and down to the shores of Chew Valley Lake. There I washed and shook out my clothes. I was dirty and famished, but too relieved to feel exhaustion any longer. It was certain that the poor terrified disciple would never report the loss of his car and risk reviving the interest of police.

I stopped at a transport cafe and ate an immense supper. They looked at me oddly, but found me just presentable enough to be served. Then, with sleep the only enemy to fight, I drove temperately back to London. At one in the morning I was in bed, my own bed, thinking myself truly free at last, for I had slammed the Gate of the Underworld behind me. But memory has no gate, or else I am not the sort of man who can close it. Whenever the call is insistent, I am still forced to go down, alone, to the darkness and find in the reality of the hunters and the hunted my defense against the dead.